Even The
SPARROWS
Have
FORGOTTEN

Even the Sparrows Have Forgotten

For SD

Books by N.C. Hayes

The Redfern Legacy

The Wayward Prince
The Queen of Reckoning

A Kingdom of Honey and Salt

Even The Sparrows Have Forgotten

1

The sights and smells of early autumn in the faerie realm were just out of reach while I remained trapped in our hot, stuffy carriage. I was crammed between the window and Gwenna, my stepsister. My stepmother, Wilda, and other stepsister, Giselle sat across from us. Their tall hair and many-layered skirts left little breathing room in the carriage, and I longed to open my window for some fresh air but knew better than to risk a gust of wind. The three of them had insisted on wearing their finest clothes for today's journey across the Kingdom of Daybreak, with their hair curled to perfection and pinned in a fashion they all claimed was popular in Stag Court, the capital. How they would know this, I had no idea, since this was the first time any of them had left our home in Sparrow Court for the last decade. We left hours before the sun was up and had only stopped twice to stretch our legs. It was late in the afternoon, and we were getting close to our destination.

"You can wipe that miserable look off your face, Margot," my stepmother said flatly while she checked her makeup in a small mirror. She had dusted the tips of her pointed ears in colored powder to match her seafoam green dress— one of the supposed capital fashions she and her daughters adopted. "We'll arrive in a few moments."

"Yes, lady," I replied.

"I'm sure I don't need to remind you of my expectations while we are guests of Prince Orist?"

"No, lady—"

"I could not avoid bringing you along, but nothing else has changed. You are to remain silent in the presence of the prince and his son, and you will assist your stepsisters in whatever they might require."

"I understand," I said with a sigh. Wilda did this often, explaining something that I'd just told her I already knew.

I could feel Wilda staring into me while I turned my gaze back to the window. I could feel her anxiety pulsing. "Your father would want you to be content," she said in the kindest voice she could muster. It was a rare thing, but occasionally my stepmother's guilt reared its head, and she would say things like this while I rolled my eyes.

"I am well aware of what my father wanted for me, my lady." I glared at her, refusing to even fake gratitude for being allowed to leave Sparrow Court for this. It was no act of kindness.

Wilda was forced by the wording of Prince Orist's invitation to bring me along. For the first time since Papa's death, fae magic had worked in my favor, but it did not grant me my freedom. My bloody tooth, which she'd stolen— or rather, had my stepsisters steal— the night my father died, still hung in a glass vial around her neck. Blood and bone. It was all that was needed to keep a human under a faerie's control, and since my mother was human, Wilda had correctly guessed that such a spell might work on me. It was an enormous risk to take. It would not protect her forever, but for the foreseeable future, Wilda held the power of Sparrow Court hostage, while I retained only my title: Lady of Sparrows. That, luckily, was the one thing she could not take from me, and it was the reason I sat suffocating next to Gwenna.

A letter arrived a week ago, on the morning of the equinox, inviting the official household of Sparrow Court to Prince Orist's manor, so that the daughters of House Brightwood could be presented for a potential marriage arrangement to Lord Ever Oakshadow, Orist's son, and a grandson of the High King of Daybreak. Even before realizing that I was meant to go along, my interest had been piqued at the mention of the lord's name. Lord Ever had been granted his position just over a decade prior and was named Lord of the Waterways— a title plucked from thin air, it would seem, to give the king's grandson something to do with his existence. He had a reputation worthy of even Sparrow Court gossip. Not for his taste in lovers, or any form of scandal, as we so often heard of the royal family and other noblefae, but for his success and popularity. A minor lord with a royal name, Ever Oakshadow's greatest supporters were the merchants and working class fae his family ruled over. It was an odd thing— admirable, I supposed—that his fortune had not come from inheritances or gifts. The lord had managed to prove wrong every gossip and doubter in Daybreak by taking his role and thriving within it. He introduced a trade system to the merchant guilds of each court, and implemented it via the connecting rivers, collecting his share, of course, on each shipment that passed through— which was practically everything these days. He had connected the faerie markets to each other through the canals, which encouraged inter-court trade in ways it never had been before. He seemed to have his hand in everything from trade, to fishing, to travel. The merchants loved Ever Oakshadow, and the nobility was confused by him. Or perhaps they were confused by someone with his titles and connections working hard enough to make his position lucrative outside of his relation to the royal family.

That relation, of course, was likely the reason for Wilda's immediate, eager response. As the only child of the High King's youngest son, Lord Ever was hardly a footnote on the royal family tree. But he had the Oakshadow name, and that was enough for Wilda to jump at the opportunity for one of her daughters to be his bride. It did not matter that Lord Ever was clever or did well in his position. It did not even matter if he had money, or how much. It only mattered that a marriage between one of her daughters and someone— anyone — from House Oakshadow put Wilda one step closer to Stag Court, the royals, and thus, higher status

The Serpent Court countryside rolled by, and I noted the difference in the trees here. Back home, the leaves remained all shades of red, orange, and gold year-round. Here, the trunks of the trees were gold or mossy green, and the leaves were shades of teal, cobalt, and azure. When our carriage passed beneath the boughs, it seemed as if the sky was just an arm's length away. In the springtime, the blues would change back to shades of purple, and I lamented the thought that I would not see it in person.

While Giselle chittered away mostly to herself, with her mother contributing the occasional grunt of approval, something caught my eye a few yards off the road. A flash of red. I blinked a few times and saw hidden in the tall grass a wide circle of red mushrooms.

"*Stop!*" I cried out. "Stop the carriage!"

"Margot, what in Aven's name—"

"There's a faerie ring out there," I said, pointing. "Please, Wilda, tell the driver to stop and let me go break it—"

"We do not have time, Margot. I will not keep the prince waiting," Wilda said.

3

"You speak so often about the things my father would have wanted, stepmother. You know he would have stopped to destroy that thing." I looked out the window again, but we were already well past the circle. I kept my eyes glued to the spot as it became smaller and smaller. I blinked a few times, trying to keep myself from crying in front of my stepsisters.

"If it is still there on the way home, we will stop and destroy it," Wilda said with a sigh. "But we are already late."

"How many humans do you think will be trapped here by the time we pass it again?" I asked without looking at her. "Two? Ten?"

"Stop with the theatrics," she huffed. "You don't know that the whole thing is even intact. Someone could have already broken the circle."

"Perhaps," I replied. "Or perhaps some humans will have their lives utterly ruined—"

"Your mother's life made quite the improvement when she came here, if my memory serves me."

"Do not speak of my mother," I snapped. I glared at her, and to my surprise she fell quiet.

My mother, Grace, was a human woman who had been trapped by a faerie ring. They are the only known portals between the faerie realm and human realm, and they only bring humans to our realm, not the other way around. Once a human has landed in Faerie, they are here for the rest of their life.

It was not always that way. Once, centuries ago, almost any fae could pop into the human realm to pay a visit, to cause mayhem, or anything in between. While humans required the help of a faerie to return home, it could be done easily. But the first Queen of Faerie, Aven, had closed the doorways between realms when her most trusted noblefae began to betray her. She cursed the four of them, and their entire bloodlines, to rule the lands of Faerie forevermore. One of them was my ancestor, the first Lady of Sparrows, ruler of Sparrow Court in the west of Daybreak. The head of House Oakshadow was cursed to become High King of Daybreak and took his seat of power in the center of the kingdom, Stag Court. To the east was Serpent Court, and to the north, beyond the mountains, was the Kingdom of Nightfall.

Queen Aven placed her curses and disappeared over a thousand years ago. No one has ever been able to reverse the magic, which meant the noble houses of Daybreak were obligated to carry out their duties to the crown, and an Oakshadow must always hold the throne.

Aven's only oversight was the faerie rings. One way or another, someone had discovered that using traveler's magic to form a portal, a method of travel taught to children in the old days, formed a doorway between the realms. Humans would wander in and be spirited away from their world to ours.

Faerie rings were banned in Daybreak, but young fae often made them as a prank, perhaps not realizing or caring how damaging they truly were. Luckily, it only took breaking the circle to ruin the portal and prevent human trapping. Such a simple act, and yet Wilda would not stop the carriage and risk three minutes' further tardiness.

"Straighten yourselves, girls," I heard Wilda say over my stream of thoughts. "I can see the manor." I followed her gaze and saw the Prince's manor home— not the Serpent Palace, but a countryside estate where the prince could entertain more intimately. It was a strange dwelling, low and wide, forming a sort of horseshoe shape made of gray brick covered in moss and vines. It was so wet here, I imagined most fae stopped trying to fight the climbing greenery on their homes and just accepted its existence.

My stepsisters smoothed their skirts and swept flyaway hairs back where they belonged. Giselle looked at her mother, who reached to readjust her necklace and praise her eldest daughter. Gwenna looked at me nervously and I gave her a nod— as much encouragement as I would offer.

Gwenna was the kinder of my stepsisters. She took part in her mother's schemes out of obligation, but took no joy from them, the way Giselle did. As much as I would prefer Gwenna's company to her sister's, I hoped for her sake that she was chosen by Ever Oakshadow. She deserved a chance to live outside the reach of her mother and sister. The poor girl had no useful skills— her mother saw to that, insisting that a true lady should be little more than a pretty face— and so she would only suit the role of a rich lord's wife, even if his title was all but fiction.

The carriage came to a stop, and my stepsisters practically shook with nerves. The door opened, and Giselle shoved past Gwenna to make her descent first. Gwenna followed, leaving me alone with Wilda, who fiddled with the vial on her necklace while she spoke. "Please, just make yourself scarce, Margot. Stand by the bags."

"Yes, Lady Wilda," I replied, and my stepmother tucked the necklace down the front of her dress before making her exit.

I waited a beat, savoring a few seconds of silence before I too climbed out of the carriage.

I did as I was told and began helping the footman with our bags. He wore a Serpent Court insignia, as the carriage had been sent by Prince Orist himself, and so he did not know who I was. Sparrow Court workers never let me pitch in, but just this once I was allowed to make myself useful and stay out of the way.

I eavesdropped while introductions were made. Wilda and Prince Orist knew each other from years prior and spent a moment kissing cheeks before the prince stepped aside and introduced Lord Ever. They looked almost nothing alike. While the prince was undoubtedly handsome, he was quite fair, with flushed skin and strawberry locks grazing his collar. He had bright, robin-blue eyes and white freckles like the spots on a deer. Lord Ever's face was sharper, with a squared jaw and high cheekbones, which made him look like he'd been carved from stone. His hair and eyes were nearly black, which complimented the dark green suit he wore, and his skin was a few shades more tanned than his father's. It occurred to me that I had no idea who Ever Oakshadow's mother was– not that having a private consort was unusual for royal fae. He must take after her.

Giselle, for all her annoying tendencies, greeted Lord Ever politely, dipping into a curtsy with her eyes pointed toward the ground. She peered up at him under her lashes when she rose, like her mother taught her, and even I had to admit she looked rather pretty. Gwenna, shy as a fawn, practically whispered her greetings before dipping down quickly. Despite his intense gaze, Lord Ever looked at Gwenna kindly, and greeted her by name. The pointed tips of her ears turned pink beneath the sage green powder she'd dusted on this morning.

"Shall we go inside?" Prince Orist suggested. "I know you've had a long day of travel so I won't bore you with too much of a tour, but I really must show you the dew pond— your companion can make her way to your suite, if that suits you. My servants will show her the way."

Wilda looked at me, and, with a shooing motion, directed me toward the manor. I made a brief show of bowing my head to all of them. To my surprise, Lord Ever dipped his chin, making a point to acknowledge me before I continued. The rest ignored me as they began their slow walk to the other end of the estate. Lord Ever offered an arm to each of my stepsisters, and as I watched them walk toward the dew pond, I silently hoped Wilda would fall in.

2

Despite the size of the manor, its layout was not at all complicated, and I found the suite easily. I wondered if this home was unique, or if the low, wide layout of the building was a common design in Serpent Court, the way tall, narrow buildings were common in Sparrow Court.

The four of us would share the suite, though I was in a small, hidden alcove, separate from my stepfamily. A section of wall blocked their view of my bed, and I was happy that they would be unable to complain about my lamp when I inevitably wanted to stay awake and read.

Wilda burst through the door just as I finished laying out all the cosmetics on the single vanity the three of them were to share. "Hurry up, we only have an *hour*—" she noticed me. "Be a dear and help Gwenna with her hair. It's a disaster." Gwenna rushed to sit on one of the beds, waiting for me to help her, even though her hair looked exactly as it had when I left them. Gwenna's face was pink, and she looked close to tears. Giselle was already sitting at the vanity, brushing out her sapphire curls— twin to her mother's— with a smug look on her face, her upturned nose crinkled with satisfaction at the sight of her miserable sister.

"I don't know why you bother," she taunted. Gwenna looked straight ahead while I began pulling the pins from her hair. "You should save your efforts for when I make you my bridesmaid. Perhaps Lord Ever's merchant friends will be in attendance at our wedding, and you can find a husband that way." Wilda shot her daughter a stern look, which was about as much as she would do to scold Giselle. Both my stepsisters knew they were expected to marry someone with a title. Even jokes about a match with a merchant were unacceptable. Gwenna

7

sniffed while I ran a comb through her hair, which was a straighter texture and more muted shade of blue than her sister's.

"Lord Ever did smile at me," Gwenna mumbled. "He would have spoken with me more if Giselle would give anyone else a chance to speak."

"I'm sure he found you charming," I said, unable to let someone feel so sorry for themselves in front of me. "There's still a whole evening to get through." Gwenna nodded. Minutes later, I managed to put a wave in her hair and let it flow simply down her back, pinning the front away with silver combs. Her dress was a rosy pink that made the flush of her cheeks stand out, and I thought she looked quite pretty. She insisted on ear powder, like Wilda and Giselle, so I found some in silver to match her combs and rubbed it on the points. Gwenna looked in the mirror and by the way she turned her head to examine herself I could tell she felt pretty too.

"I suppose that will have to do," Wilda said with a sigh as she looked her younger daughter up and down. The light that had lived so briefly in Gwenna's eyes went out. "Come along, we must get going." My stepmother ushered the girls out the door. Before following, she added to me, "There will be a plate for you in the kitchen with the prince's servants. You're dismissed for the night."

"Yes, stepmother."

I waited about an hour, enjoying the quiet and dozing on the bed before my stomach growled long and loud enough that I could not ignore it. The kitchen servants were kind and made room at their table for me to join them while I ate. They made small talk, and a couple of the cooks tried to convince me to bet on which of my stepsisters Lord Ever would choose. They laughed when I refused, calling me a poor sport, and one of the maids encouraged me to ignore them. When I'd eaten my fill, I asked if anyone knew where I might find a place to read. The maid told me how to find the library and assured me I would be left alone. "The staff hardly ever go in, and the prince is occupied. No one will bother you." I thanked her, and before I left she pressed a large goblet of berrywine into my hand with a wink.

I found the library easily and slipped inside. The fireplace crackled but failed to give me enough light to see the whole room. I found matches next to a lantern and lit it, carrying it with me to illuminate the titles stamped in gold on the leather spines. I drifted beyond the memoirs and histories that overwhelmed the shelves, finding a small section of novels and legends on a low corner shelf.

I made my selection— a volume of children's fables— then found my drink and plopped myself happily on one of the sofas. It was more peace than I'd had in months— perhaps years— and more than I was likely to have for some time.

I was nose deep in a story about a wicked witch corrupting a beehive when I heard footsteps shuffle into the library and the door shut with a dull *thud*. How long had I been reading? Was the party over? I poked my head over the back of the sofa and nearly yelped in surprise when I saw Lord Ever leaning against the closed double-doors.

"Shit," he said upon seeing my face appear. "Sorry, I thought I was alone."

He moved to open the door but stopped when I said, "Don't—!" He turned around, looking puzzled. "I'm sorry, my lord, I only mean that this is your home. I should be the one to leave."

He made a noise that I might have mistaken for a laugh if he did not look so grim. "No need." He walked to a cupboard and pulled out a decanter and a pair of short glasses. "Drink?"

"No, thank you, my lord, I have one." Lord Ever poured himself some of the liquor and knocked it all back in one go before pouring another and approaching me to sit on the opposite end of the sofa.

"Are you hiding from the party as well?" he asked, putting his feet up on the small table before us and crossing one ankle over the other. His arm rested on the back of the sofa, and a gold earring I had not noticed before dangled from his ear, glimmering in the light of the fireplace as he shifted, getting himself comfortable. If Lord Ever was in a state of unease, I would never know it.

I straightened, blushing slightly when I realized I was still lounging on his furniture as if I owned it. I smoothed my skirt and said, "I'm not hiding, my lord. I am not meant to be at the party, so I found myself a drink and somewhere else to be."

"Where are you meant to be, if not at the party your household was invited to?"

"Home. My household is..." I let my words drift to silence. "My stepmother and stepsisters are the ones who are meant to be here." Lord Ever gave me a peculiar look, then turned his attention to the book sitting open in my lap.

"And what did you find to fill your time this evening?" I picked it up and showed him the cover. "Children's stories?"

I shrugged. "Better than the histories and memoirs of a thousand years' worth of stuffed-up faelords," I blurted. Almost immediately I covered my mouth, cursing the wine in my glass for loosening my lips. Lord Ever barked a laugh.

"I cannot say I blame you," he replied, and relief washed over me. The last thing I wanted was to anger a lord in his own home— or, his father's, anyway. He extended his hand. "Ever Oakshadow."

"Margaret Brightwood," I replied, accepting the handshake. When he let go, Lord Ever blinked at me.

"Margaret?" he asked, and I clenched my teeth together before nodding once, slowly. He considered, looking me up and down a few more times.

"...What?"

"Nothing, nothing. So, since stuffy histories and memoirs do not interest you, what do you normally like to read?"

We dove into a discussion of the books we liked and which we hated. He told me of the hours of lessons he was required to attend as a child and that he'd read nearly every one of the books on the shelves here in his father's summer estate— which, he informed me, did not compare to the libraries at either the Serpent or Stag Palaces. I told him of my collection back home, containing mostly adventure novels and love stories my mother enjoyed. When my goblet ran dry, he gave me a glass of the same liquor he drank. By the time an hour was gone, he'd had three full glasses and did not appear the least bit drunk. I, however, was feeling rather tipsy, swaying as I perched beside him on the sofa.

When a silence overcame us, Lord Ever looked me over thoughtfully and asked, "Tell me, were you ever going to announce yourself as Lady of Sparrows or were you going to try and pretend that you're nothing more than a ladies' maid for this entire visit?"

I blanched. "I'm not pretending, my lord."

"Lady Margaret, I don't know what game you're playing—"

"It is no game, my lord." I sighed, defeated. "I know better than to tell strangers of the goings-on in my stepmother's home."

"You are not simply telling, I am asking," he said in a dry, matter-of-fact way. "If it makes things easier, I could order you to reveal why you are not announcing your title. As Lord of the Waterways, it's well within my rights to know which members of the nobility are entering this estate." I swallowed. He was probably joking, but I still nodded. "Go on then. Tell me. I command it."

I swallowed again. My throat was suddenly dry. I gulped down the rest of my drink and set the glass aside before speaking. "I assume, if you knew me so quickly, that you must have known my father."

"I met Lord Thorn on a handful of occasions, yes."

"You likely met my mother then and would know the circumstances of my heritage."

"There is no law that says noble born half-fae must relinquish their titles."

"True," I agreed. "But there are also few laws that prevent one usurping their power." Lord Ever stared, waiting for me to elaborate. Instead of fumbling with my words, I hooked my finger into the corner of my mouth, dragging downward to reveal a missing molar. "I may only be half, but human blood still runs in my veins," I explained. "Just after my father died, my stepmother ordered her daughters to attack me. They beat my face until they knocked a tooth loose. In my anger, when I stood, I spat it and a mouthful of blood at their feet." It took a few seconds before Lord Ever sat back fully against the sofa.

"Blood and bone," he murmured.

"Yes," I said stiffly. "I am at Wilda's mercy for as long as she wants to keep me. I was stripped of my power in an instant. She holds it hostage now and lets the whole of Daybreak believe whatever rumors they've concocted about my fate: that I am ill, or insane, driven mad by my parents' deaths so close to one another. I have nothing left but my title. I am Lady of Sparrows, but I do not hold Sparrow Court. The servants, the farm hands... They know who I am. They try to do as much as they can for me. But my stepmother is their mistress now."

Lord Ever looked at me with what might pass as pity for just a moment before turning to pick up his drink once again. "And I'm meant to marry one of these monsters."

"For what it's worth, I'd pick Gwenna," I said flatly. "She's not very interesting, but she's also not cruel of her own accord. Her mother and sister put her up to things. She's scared of winding up like me, I suspect." Perhaps becoming Lady of the Waterways would be good for Gwenna. It would give her some power. Lord Ever would give her a good life and plenty of children to look after. And I would have a powerful brother-by-law who seemed to like me well enough— or at least pity me.

"I'll keep that in mind," he said irritably before looking up at the clock on the wall. "It seems I've been here long enough to thoroughly insult my guests and irritate the prince. I should return to the party." We both stood, and this time when he reached for my hand, rather than shaking it, he pressed a brief kiss to the back of it. "My lady, it was a pleasure." I stiffened.

"The pleasure was mine, my lord." I hoped he would not continue calling me *lady* if we saw each other again. Not even the gods would be able to help me if Wilda heard him.

I managed to make my way back to my quarters without stumbling. I was not used to drinking at all, let alone a lord's private liquor. My stomach churned and I found myself bent over the toilet, vomiting as quietly as I could manage. When I was finished, I found the sink. I rinsed out my mouth and splashed water on my face. I didn't bother to undress and simply collapsed on a bed, falling asleep before I could manage to kick off my shoes.

3

Something smacked me in the face, leaving a lingering sting on my cheek as my eyes fluttered open.

"Wake *up!*" Wilda commanded. Groggily, I sat up in the bed and rubbed at my eyes. "Give me back my shoe." I reached for the thin leather slipper she'd thrown at me and gave it to her. She hit me in the head with it once more before stomping away toward the bathroom, grumbling to herself.

"You slept on *my* bed last night, Margot," Gwenna complained from the vanity seat where she brushed her hair. "You didn't even take your shoes off."

"Sorry," I mumbled, rubbing again at my eyes. "Didn't realize—"

"You reeked of booze when we came in," Giselle taunted. "Did you sneak off and get drunk with the help?"

"I wasn't—"

"When *I'm* Lady of the Waterways, my staff will not be permitted to be so foolish," Giselle continued.

"Who says it will be you?" Gwenna snapped. "I'll remind you he danced with me last night as well. He complimented my dress."

"He was being polite— Lord Ever danced with mother too, and it's not like he's going to marry her."

"When will he choose?" I asked my stepsisters.

"A note came with our tea this morning," Wilda answered for them as she emerged from the bathroom. "Lord Ever will announce his choice at midday, during a luncheon in the garden. Why aren't you dressed yet?" Her words were sharper than usual.

"I did not realize I was required to be, stepmother," I replied. "Am I going somewhere?"

13

She reached forward and flicked me in the forehead, making me flinch. "Don't be smart with me, girl. Whether I like it or not, you're to join us for the announcement. Now get dressed, we're due in the garden in two hours." Wilda stomped away to sit on her bed with the hand mirror and began applying too much rouge to her cheeks.

"This should be a treat for you, Margot," Gwenna said earnestly. She dropped her voice. "If you want, you can come work for me when I get settled."

"Don't be stupid, Gwenna," Giselle hissed. "You know mother would never allow that." Gwenna shrugged and I turned to dig through my trunk for something suitable to wear, and to hide the rage that threatened to boil over.

We met our hosts at the edge of a garden path that we would all walk together to reach the clearing where the luncheon had been set up. Lord Ever and Prince Orist greeted my stepmother and stepsisters as they had the day before. Today, Lord Ever met my eyes. He gave me a nod and the briefest of tight-lipped smiles. Thank the gods he did not deign to speak with me. I would not survive the carriage ride back to Sparrow Court if he did.

I lingered at the back of the group as we walked. I was joined by a girl, who I assumed to be a servant.

"Hello," she said warmly after we'd been walking for a moment. "I'm Rhea. I work for Lord Ever. He suggested I walk with you today, is that alright?"

"I'm Margot," I told her with a nod. "Be my guest."

"Happy to meet you, Margot. This is all so exciting, don't you think?"

"I suppose," I sighed. "It's nice to be outside on a day like today, anyway."

"I never thought my lord would choose a bride, and now, here we are!" Rhea was practically giddy. I almost felt bad for not caring about anything beyond the entrée. Rhea continued, dropping her voice to a whisper. "Did you hear, the union is going to be Bound?"

"Is it really?" I asked flatly.

Soulbinding was not unheard of. Plenty of noblefae Bound themselves to their spouses upon marriage. It helped make arranged unions more palatable to those involved. They'd perform blood magic during the wedding ceremony to mimic the primal mating bonds of the ancient fae and encourage consummation, after which the pair would be Soulbound— their very souls linked until the end of their days.

Commonfae only Bound themselves when truly, deeply in love before marriage— if they could afford the fee for a High Priestess to complete the ceremony, that is.

"Yes. Lord Ever informed the prince this morning of his decision and His Highness approved."

"Do you know who he's chosen?" I asked.

"I don't." She seemed irritated by that. "Only he and the prince know. I couldn't get it out of him at breakfast."

"Get it out of him?"

"Oh, I pestered him of course, but Lord Ever would not budge. He said it had to remain a surprise."

"Oh— of course." Our conversation dropped as we approached the clearing, and I wondered what sort of punishment Wilda would come up with for me if I ever dared to pester her for information.

There were two tables set for dining. One was long and rectangular, with settings for the lord, the prince, Wilda, Gwenna, and Giselle. The other was small and circular, set with only two places, for myself and Rhea. I looked over at the large table and had to hold back my laughter at the sight of Gwenna and Giselle taking their places on either side of Lord Ever, both blabbering away while he wore a mask of polite indifference.

Bottles of wine appeared on their table and when I turned back to mine, to my surprise I found a glass sitting before me. I took a sip before glancing at Lord Ever, who looked quickly toward me. I raised my glass slightly in his direction, to give my thanks, and he turned back to his conversation. A moment later, plates of food appeared in front of us.

"Oh, this is lovely," Rhea said mostly to herself. There were small platters of various cheeses, fruit, and olives, a basket of fresh bread, and roast chicken that smelled of sage and butter served with root vegetables. Rhea and I served ourselves and ate quietly, the pair of us coming to a silent agreement that we wanted to hear anything being said at the big table.

Wilda and the prince were chatting away, while Gwenna and Giselle took turns talking over one another as Lord Ever ate his food and pretended to listen.

"You think he'll make himself happy with one of them?" I asked Rhea quietly.

"As they are? Likely not," she replied, whispering as well. "Perhaps that is the reason for the Soulbinding."

"Perhaps."

When everyone was finished eating, the plates cleared themselves, leaving the tabletops empty except for the linens and glasses. A few minutes of conversation continued, until Lord Ever stood from his seat and cleared his throat.

"Thank you all for joining Prince Orist and myself for this excellent meal and... riveting conversation." I pressed my lips together, trying not to smile at the sarcasm. It appeared my stepfamily did not notice it. "We all know the intended purpose of this visit has been to introduce the possibility of joining myself with Sparrow Court in marriage. I am delighted to say that after meeting you all, I have chosen my bride." I watched Gwenna and Giselle join hands across the table. I could only see Gwenna's face from where I sat, and her eyes looked shiny. No matter which sister Lord Ever chose, they would be separated for the first time in their lives. I had to admit, the thought was rather sad. I might've felt sorry for them if they weren't so awful in every other regard. "Should she accept my proposal, we shall be wed before sunset, and we shall feast tonight, all of us together again in this very manor." I could feel my stepfamily's anxiety pouring from the big table and I wondered if Lord Ever simply enjoyed the suspense or if he was stalling. "And so, it is my great honor to ask for the hand of Margaret Brightwood, Lady of Sparrows."

I felt the blood leave my face as everyone's attention turned to me.

My stepmother shot to her feet, outraged. "The choice was meant to be between my daughters! This cannot be!"

Lord Ever ignored her, staring directly at me. "My lady, your answer?"

"I—" I stammered, trying to form words. I could feel Wilda's eyes on me, knowing that if she had the ability, she would have set me aflame the second he said my name. The discomfort was almost too much to bear. I could not begin to imagine what it would be like on the carriage ride home. Would she lock me in my rooms for a month? A year?

Then it dawned on me that I did not have to find out.

I stood from my seat. Despite my shaking hands, I took a deep breath and folded them in front of me before saying softly, "I accept."

4

Everything that happened next was a blur.

Wilda immediately started ranting to the prince that she had been lured here under false pretenses. Gwenna was crying softly while Giselle wore a mask of rage that I knew to mean that she was thoroughly embarrassed. Lord Ever approached me and leaned in as if he meant to kiss my cheek. Instead, he murmured, "Go with Rhea. She'll get you what you need. We'll speak later." Then he was gone, walking swiftly back down the path we'd all entered from. I watched as he disappeared, stunned that I'd just agreed to this.

Rhea tugged on my arm. "My lady, we should go while the rest are occupied." I nodded and followed. I would not want to be on the receiving end of my stepmother's wrath when she finished with Prince Orist.

Rhea took me back to the manor and into a suite that I had not seen the previous day. There, she sat me in a cushioned vanity seat and began unwrapping my braid. I cringed, noticing it was quite frizzy. She shook it out, as if getting an idea of what she was working with.

"I don't understand why he asked me," I said after a moment. "We only spoke for a few minutes...he doesn't know anything about me except for my name. The books I like."

"If I had to make a guess, my lady, I would say that was enough." She bid me to stand, then began loosening the laces on the back of my dress. "My lord is a good judge of character. He could see you for the kind person you are, and your stepsisters for their... qualities. He made his choice, and you've accepted. You'll make a lovely couple." She let my dress fall to the floor, leaving me in nothing but a shift. She slipped a silk robe over my shoulders and told me to sit again. "I'll

17

draw a bath and let you wash before we—"

The door burst open and my stepmother stormed in, marching right up and slapping me across the face. "*How dare you!* You little *thief!* You *scum!*" She shrieked, hitting me again before Rhea forced her body between us.

"Lady Wilda, you must go," Rhea said firmly.

"*You* do not speak to *me*, maid! You do not give me orders!"

"I act with the permission of my lord. You must leave."

Wilda ignored her and turned her attention back to me, seething as she stared over Rhea's shoulder. "How did you do it then? How did you trick Lord Ever?" Giselle and Gwenna stood quietly in the doorway, turning their eyes downward.

"I didn't—"

"When you disappeared last night, where did you go?"

"I went to the library," I admitted quietly. "We spoke for a few minutes. He offered me a drink—"

She barked a humorless laugh, cutting me off. "So, you whored yourself out to the Lord of the Waterways to raise your station and bring ruin to the good names of your stepsisters. You selfish, greedy little bi—" Wilda's ranting was cut off when Rhea, without touching her, pushed her hand forward, throwing my stepmother out of the room and slamming the door behind her. I heard the lock latch itself over the sound of Wilda's following tantrum. Rhea turned her attention back to me.

"My lady, I am going to step out and deal with that. I trust you can figure out the bath on your own?"

"I— yes. I can. Thank you, Rhea." I tried not to sound as shaken as I felt. My face stung as I held my palm to it.

"Just ring the bell if you need anything," she said, and then she was gone.

I hurried into the bathroom and shut the door behind me, latching it soundly before letting a shuddering breath escape me. I allowed myself just a few seconds of panic before setting myself to the task at hand. Nothing was final until the ceremony. I would not be free of my stepfamily until then. I had to keep it together and not falter in any regard. I let the robe fall and took off my shift before letting the tub fill. I examined the cart of bottles that sat beside the tub and selected a rosemary and plum bath oil which I poured into the steaming water. It turned a light purple color, and I stepped in.

I did not have time to lounge in the tub as I would have liked. It had been several years, but I remembered well the time and effort it took to prepare for any sort of feast, let alone a wedding. I scrubbed my hair gently, rinsed it, then decided I'd better do it twice. I applied a hair oil that smelled of rosehips and by the time I was stepping out of the now lukewarm tub, I could hear Rhea calling me to join her in the next room.

It took nearly two hours for Rhea to do my hair and another hour to do the makeup. I had not worn any since the night before Papa died, and had no idea how to do it myself, so I let her. Almost as soon as she'd finished there was a knock on the door. Rhea answered and collected a box from a delivery boy before shutting and latching the door once again. "I hope you don't mind, my lady, but I sent for a dress on your behalf."

"Oh," I said, having forgotten that I would indeed need a wedding dress. The one I wore to the garden today was the finest I owned, if I didn't count the trunk of my mother's ball gowns back at Sparrow Court. "Thank you, Rhea."

"Of course, my lady. I think it will suit you nicely." She set the box down on the bed and opened it, revealing an amethyst gown. I removed my robe and Rhea helped me step into it. I slipped my arms into the sheer, flowy sleeves while she laced up the back. In the mirror, I looked prettier than I had ever seen myself. My heart ached that Mama and Papa were not here to see me this way. Then again, if they were, it would not have come to this. "Oh, it is exactly as I pictured," Rhea gushed. Her sentimentality was short lived, however, when she glanced at the clock and said, "Quickly now, we must get going!" She helped me into the shoes that matched the dress, and we were off to my wedding.

I was left to linger outside of a pair of double doors that led to a ballroom, where the ceremony would take place. Rhea dropped me off then hurried away, letting me know she would see me later. I stood, wringing my hands, terrified that any second, Wilda would come around the corner and finish what she started.

A door opened on the far end of the hallway, and I jumped. I saw that it was Lord Ever. For a second, I was relieved, but then new anxiety set in. I was about to marry him. I picked at my nail bed while he approached.

"Hello," he said when he reached me.

"Hello," I replied nervously. He took my hand and kissed it formally.

"You look beautiful, Lady Margaret," he said stiffly, though his voice was not unkind.

"So do you— I mean, handsome—not that one wouldn't consider you beautiful, I just meant...You look handsome, my lord," I stammered and felt my face go red. He gave me a brief, reassuring smile.

"You can call me Ever in private," he said. "No need for titles between spouses I suppose. Shall I call you Margaret?"

"Margot," I corrected. "I prefer Margot."

"Margot it is then," Ever promised. He sighed deeply. "Shall we get on with it then?" I nodded and took the arm he offered. "Deep breath," he murmured. I took one at the same time he did, and when we let them out, the doors before us dissolved into nothing.

We faced the nearly empty ballroom. At the far end of it stood a High Priestess. To her left stood Prince Orist, and to her right were four chairs. Three of them were occupied by my stepmother and stepsisters, while the fourth sat empty, waiting for the prince to sit.

When we arrived before the High Priestess, we waited in silence while she observed the pair of us.

"My lord, please declare your name and your intention for this ceremony," she said when she finally spoke.

"I am Ever Oakshadow, Lord of the Waterways. It is my intention to wed and be Bound to Margaret Brightwood, Lady of Sparrows."

The High Priestess turned her attention to me. "My lady, your name and intention?"

I swallowed. "I am Margaret Brightwood, Lady of Sparrows," I said softly. The words felt foreign on my tongue. "It is my intention to wed... and be Bound to Ever Oakshadow, Lord of the Waterways."

She bid us to face one another and kneel while joining hands. "And do you both agree to this union?"

"I do," said Ever.

"I do," I said.

"Then let us begin."

Much of the ceremony was simply listening to the priestess chant in an ancient language I did not know. After what seemed like a long time, the priestess presented us with a pair of rings that I had never seen. They were simple gold bands that I imagined Prince Orist must have picked out when planning for this visit, just in case. Ever took the one meant for me and slipped it onto my finger before I did the same with his. The priestess, still speaking in the old tongue, then presented a jeweled box. She opened it, revealing a knife with a silver handle.

"The Blood Binding," Ever said to me under his breath. "Ready?"

I nodded, though I was sure I looked terrified.

The High Priestess gave me the knife, and I took it despite not having any idea what I should do with it. Ever came to my rescue by presenting me with his open hand and wiggling his first finger. I took the hint and slid the knife across his fingertip, just deep enough to allow it to bleed freely. Ever then took the knife from me and did the same. Then we were to place our fingertips, in unison, on each other's forehead, then each cheek, then chin, dragging a line down the front of our necks until we reached the breastbone. We then took turns smearing what was left on each other's eyelids and mouths, staining our lips as if the blood were makeup. The priestess was speaking through all of it, and Ever murmured a rough translation while he drew on my face with his blood:

"Our blood we shall bind.
Our souls we shall bind.
Stitched as one,
'til the stars go dark
and the sun leaves the sky."

His blood tingled where it lay on my skin. As we finished, the High Priestess said something else before staring at us expectantly. I turned my attention back to Ever, who looked apologetic.

"I'm supposed to kiss you now," he explained in a whisper.

"Oh," I whispered back. "That's alright."

I thought he mouthed *sorry* before leaning forward and placing his hand on my cheek. He brushed his lips against mine and immediately, warmth spread from where our blood joined on our mouths through the rest of my body, down my limbs and into my fingers and toes. A sharp pain pierced me— not quite in my chest, but somewhere deeper. It was like being poked with a needle, though just as quickly as I felt it, the sensation was gone. He lingered for only a few seconds before we parted, and I could not tell from looking at him if he felt the same thing I did. My blood was gone from his face. It had been absorbed by his skin, and was a part of him forever now, as his blood had been absorbed by me. Ever gave me that tight-lipped smile again before retaking my hands in his own. The High Priestess, switching back to the common tongue, then declared us to be husband and wife. Prince Orist clapped loudly and stood from his seat, while my stepmother and stepsisters silently fumed. Ever helped me to stand, and I felt quite wobbly, having sat on my knees for so long, but maintained my balance while we made our way back to the double doors and out of the ballroom.

5

Rhea was waiting for us in the hallway. She held a handkerchief and looked as if she'd been crying. Quickly she tucked it into her sleeve and greeted us with a curtsy. "Congratulations my lord. My lady."

"Thank you, Rhea," Ever said. "Is everything set for the feast?"

"Yes, my lord," she said.

"And our suite is ready for tonight?"

"I'm on my way to ensure that it is."

"Good." He reached forward to squeeze her shoulder. "I cannot thank you enough."

"It's an honor, my lord. I just wish your mother were here with us." Ever stiffened a bit.

"Me too, Rhea." He looked down at me. "Shall we?"

I nodded and waved to Rhea before we parted again. Ever led me down a hallway, to another set of doors. Behind them was a dining hall, with a few long tables set up inside. Thirty or so faeries I'd never met were already seated. They laughed and talked while ale and wine were poured. Scattered applause and whooping over the top of the noise broke out. Ever nodded to a few of them as we passed by, making our way to the head table, which held four chairs. We took the pair in the middle, and I blanched when Prince Orist and my stepmother sat on the either side of us. I could feel Wilda's hatred radiating from her. I shifted in my seat, scooting slightly closer to Ever if it meant being further away from her.

Plates were placed in front of us, and before I could pick up my fork, a short hobgoblin from the kitchens placed a new goblet before me. I thanked him and reached for it, sniffing the contents.

"It's mead," Ever said, leaning in so I could hear him. "From

Sparrow Court. I thought you might like a taste of home today, so I sent for it."

I was stunned. I had not tasted Sparrow Court mead in years. When my father was still alive, honey and mead were our main exports. My fingers grazed the base of the goblet. "Thank you, my lord," I told him. "You are very kind." I took a sip and nearly cried when I tasted the honey wine on my lips. It indeed tasted like home. I had to blink a few times to regain my composure.

We ate and drank for the next hour. Dinner drew quickly to a close as the sun went down, and just as I was beginning to wonder when the dancing and revelry would begin, the guests began to file out.

"Rhea will take you to make your preparations," Ever said in my ear. "She'll bring you to my suite when you're ready." He bowed his head, kissed my hand, and then he was gone.

"Come along, my lady." Rhea stood beside me, though I had not seen her approach. "Before your stepmother notices you're alone." I nearly leapt to my feet and scurried along behind her.

When we got back to the room where I had dressed for the ceremony, Rhea bid me to strip back down to my shift. She undid all her work on my hair, and with a wave of her hand, removed the makeup from my face. It was simple magic, but even now I found myself jealous of it. My human blood meant I had not been born with magic in my veins. Only the extended lifespan and general appearance of fae features were passed to me from my father at birth. Upon his death I held the powerful magic of Sparrow Court for only a few minutes before Wilda's curse took hold. I barely felt it, and only made one command with it, but it felt as if something was missing from my bones ever since. Someday I would get it back, but for now I was powerless.

Rhea drew another bath and instructed me to wash thoroughly and swiftly, without wetting my hair. When I finished and emerged from the tub, she used a dropper to place rose oil on my skin, and assisted me in rubbing it in before helping me into a white silk nightdress with a matching robe that tied around the waist with a wide belt. She brought my hair forward, in front of my shoulders, and admired her work for a moment before telling me to sit. "Now," she said while I perched on the edge of my seat. "You may have been a bit young when your mother passed for her to have had this conversation with you, and I doubt it would have occurred to your stepmother to have it. My lord is not a cruel man, and you should not be scared of him, but I know that a young lady of your upbringing— on her wedding night might be— er— startled, by— "

"Rhea." I held up my hand to stop her. She was blushing furiously. "Thank you. But I know what sex is. My mother and I had some frank discussions."

"Thank the gods," Rhea said, sighing. She nearly laughed. "I know sometimes the noblefae can be a bit prudish with their daughters. I worried you might have been left in the dark, and I couldn't let you go to my lord without knowing what to expect."

"You are kind," I told her. "I will admit I'm nervous. But, after... everything, the Bond will be in place and I won't care anymore, right?"

"That is what they say," Rhea replied. "I am not Soulbound, lady, so I could not tell you with certainty how it all feels."

"I suppose I'm about to find out." I swallowed. "Shall we?" We rose to our feet and Rhea led me out of the room and down a dim hallway. No one else was in sight, which I was grateful for. I would not be able to stand it if Wilda were watching me walk to my first encounter with my husband.

"Here you are," Rhea said, stepping aside when we reached a lone door. "I'll leave you now."

"Thank you for everything, Rhea."

"It was a pleasure, my lady." And then she was gone.

I took a deep breath and raised my shaking fist to knock twice. A pause. "Come in," Ever said. I saw him immediately, standing before a fireplace with his back turned to me. His wedding clothes were gone, and he now wore a pair of loose black pants and a slightly oversized white shirt that as I approached, I could see was open at the top, revealing a muscled chest. The clothes did not look particularly special, but they were new and richly made. He had a glass in his hand and drained the rest of its contents. I stood beside him while he refilled his own glass and poured into a fresh one, as he had the previous night. He handed the new drink to me. My breath caught when I saw his face. He had been handsome before, but now, with the effects of the Blood Bond in place, he was absolutely striking. The firelight made his skin glow and his eyes seemed to smolder.

"Cheers," Ever said, and tapped the rim of his glass against mine before taking a drink and looking me over. "Look at you," he added, sounding exasperated. He took the edge of my robe's belt between his fingers. "They have you all wrapped up like a present." I drank from my own glass and found my hands still shaking. I nearly sloshed liquor down my front, and Ever dropped the ribbon quickly. "I'm not going to hurt you," he said.

I nodded. "I know."

"No, you don't." He sighed. "But it is a promise anyway. Now finish your drink. We should get to bed." He knocked back the rest of his drink, and before I did the same, I wondered how many he'd had before I arrived. I swallowed down the burning in my throat and left the empty glass on the mantle.

Ever waved his hand and all the lights except for the fireplace went out. He crossed the room, and I watched him discard his shirt before climbing in on one side of the bed. I stood by the other side, waiting for just a second to gather my nerves before shedding my robe. I hung it on the back of a nearby chair before quickly pulling back the blankets, sitting down, and covering myself again. I took a deep breath and waited to feel Ever's hands reach for me, to stroke my leg or remove the blankets from my lap, but it never happened. Instead, my new husband rolled to face the opposite direction, pulled the blankets up over his body, and said nothing else.

I wondered if I should reach out for him. Would he prefer me to make the first move? Or was that unladylike? Was I so awful to look at that he needed a moment to prepare himself before he could attempt this? I thought of the soft flesh that pouched on my stomach and hips, and the oversized bust that threatened to spill out of any neckline that I did not properly alter. These were human features, so unlike the lithe, angular bodies of full-blooded fae. Was Ever disgusted? If we did not consummate, the Soulbinding would not be completed, and what then? Would he change his mind, and send me back to Sparrow Court? I wanted to ask him what he would like me to do, but worse than my nerves about my wedding night was my fear of him spelling out his rejection of me. Perhaps he was being kind, letting us wait until he took me to his home, so that such a sensitive moment would not have to take place under the same roof as Wilda. I chose to let that be my final thought on the matter, banishing my worries as best I could as I lay down completely and pulled the covers to my chin.

6

I woke to a shifting on the mattress, and, suddenly remembering where I was, tensed my whole body, waiting for Ever's touch. Instead, I felt him stand up, so I turned over, and finally heard the soft knocking that must have pulled him from sleep. He did not bother putting his shirt back on, and when he answered the door, he only opened it a crack. "Yes?"

"His Highness Prince Orist has asked me to see if there is anything you might need, my lord," said a scratchy, high-pitched voice from the darkened hallway.

"Only privacy," Ever replied. "Though I imagine you also have instructions to report back to the prince what you saw, is that right?"

"... yes, my lord."

"Here." He opened the door completely, giving the visitor the full view of the suite. I squeezed my eyes shut and pretended to sleep. "If you require nothing else, I ask that you leave us. My wife needs her rest."

"Of course, my lord. Many apologies. And congrat—" Ever shut the door before the servant could finish.

"You can sleep for a few more hours," he said when he got back into bed. "It's still dark out."

"Alright," I replied in a smaller voice than I'd meant to.

"Do you need anything?"

"No, thank you."

"We'll leave after breakfast," Ever said. "I've already sent Rhea to prepare."

"Oh," I said. "Good." We were quiet again, and I began to doze in the way that makes time seem too fast. I blinked, or so it seemed, and the inky sky through the window became pink and gray. I blinked again and it was the brightest blue. Birdsong met my ears, as did Ever's movements through the room while he readied himself.

I still felt exhausted when I sat up completely, keeping the blanket over my lap. Ever was digging through a trunk with one hand while he held a steaming cup of tea in the other. "There's a kettle on the table," he announced without looking at me. "The tea is black. If you prefer lemongrass or peppermint, it can be sent for."

"Black is fine, thank you." While his back was turned, I stood, donned my robe, and tied it tightly at the waist before crossing the room to find the kettle. I filled the pretty cup covered in hand-painted lavender blossoms and added a bit of cream and thick honey before taking the first taste. It was stale, but it would do for now.

I sipped my tea, watching Ever while he continued his search for whatever it was. He gave up on the trunk after a few minutes and threw open the doors of the wardrobe. "Aha!" he exclaimed, and reached for something at the bottom, beneath the hems of old coats and moth-eaten gowns. It was a simple wooden box with a brass latch, not even a lock, which he brought to where I was sitting. "Perfect," Ever said when he opened it. He drained his cup and set it aside before pulling out a small dagger in a leather sheath. "Will you join me?" He walked back to the bed, waiting at the side I'd slept on.

Slowly, I followed, quite confused as to what he could be doing. When I reached him, he moved the blankets and took my left hand in his own, turning it so my palm faced the ceiling. My eyes lingered on our wedding rings and I began thinking how strange it seemed to be wearing one, so I was hardly paying attention when Ever said, "Quick pinch," before he dragged the tip of his blade down the length of my palm.

"*Ouch!*" I cried out, but before I could properly swear at him, Ever moved my hand to hover over the spot I slept on, and squeezed, producing droplets of blood that landed on the white sheets, staining them with bright crimson. Then, as quickly as he'd cut me, Ever ran his finger back over my palm, and the cut disappeared along with my dripping blood.

"Apologies." He lay the blanket back on top of the mess he'd made.

"What the hell was that for?" I snapped, snatching my hand away.

A knock sounded on the door. "That'll be our breakfast," Ever said. He left me where I stood and went to answer it. A pair of tiny servants entered, balancing a covered tray between them which they shakily arranged on the table near the kettle. Ever motioned for me to sit. "Come, darling, you should have something to eat." He shot me a look while the faeries were turned away, and, despite my confusion and anger, I took the seat he indicated. He sat beside me and pulled the lid, revealing a platter of honey cakes, fruit, sausages, and soft cheese. Ever filled a plate and gave it to me before making his own. I ate slowly, and tried to watch the maids straighten up the room, but they always seemed to be just out of my line of vision— a feature of their magic, I guessed, to make them less noticeable to their employers. It was impossible not to notice, though, when they began to make the bed. One pulled back the blanket to spread it properly, and the look on her furry face paired with her pointed ears standing straight clearly meant she took note of the stained sheet. She pointed it out to her companion, and waved her hand over the stain, making it disappear entirely. As soon as they were finished, they both scurried through the door and out of sight once again. Ever waved his own hand and I felt wards shift into place.

"You don't speak to your servants?" I asked when the door shut.

"They're the prince's servants, and they don't want to be spoken to," Ever replied. He bit into a honey cake slathered with cinnamon jam. Once he swallowed, he added, "They'll be paid handsomely when we leave, don't worry."

We ate in silence for a few minutes, but I couldn't stomach much more than a few polite bites. "I've angered you," I said quietly.

"Not at all."

"I know that I'm probably not what you're... used to—"

"Margot, it's nothing like that," Ever said.

"Then—" I threw my napkin onto my plate. "What is *happening*?"

"I am sorry for the confusion," he said. "There wasn't an opportunity to explain until now. No one will be lingering now that they believe we are Soulbound."

"Explain what, exactly?"

"My plan to serve both our needs without succumbing to the prince's will," Ever replied. I sat back in my seat before gesturing for him to continue. "I am compelled to follow the prince's orders. He commanded me to marry, and for there to be a Binding ceremony during the wedding. There was no getting around that. I've delayed this for more than a year, meeting with the daughters and families of every lord in Serpent Court. Once the invitation was sent to Sparrow Court, I was told I must choose this time. I was dreading the thought of being Soulbound to one of Wilda's daughters, but could not see a way out of it, until I ran into you in the library, and realized who you were. No one in any court had heard news of Thorn Brightwood's daughter since before his death."

"Oh," I said, deflating a bit. "So, it was my title."

"I cannot say that your title is not appealing, but no," Ever explained. "It was your ability to *lie*, Margot. Once I understood you to be Thorn and Grace's daughter, I knew you could be my salvation."

I felt the color drain from my face. "Because you've somehow figured out that half-fae can lie," I nearly whispered. It was not a well-known fact that half-fae can lie. Full-blooded fae could not. My parents had always instructed me to keep that ability to myself. I tried to keep my words as close to the truth as possible most of the time, so much so that I was not sure that even Wilda knew about it. But Ever either already knew or had caught me in an untruth.

"Yes."

"So, you intend to use me for your dirty work," I said. "Deceiving merchants, your father, and whoever else you wish?"

"I only require one lie from you," he replied calmly. "Let the world believe we are Soulbound. If asked, tell them of your perfect ceremony, and blush when you mention your magical wedding night. Act as if you are devoted to me, even if you hate me."

"And why would I do such a thing?"

"For the same reason you said yes to my proposal. To secure your freedom." I cocked an eyebrow at him. "You were willing to marry and Bind your soul to a stranger to escape your stepmother. It seems you understand that outside the borders of Sparrow Court, her curse has no effect on you. If it is nothing more than blood and bone she has of yours, the longer you are gone the weaker her curse will be. Her hold will die out completely in five years' time, by even the most conservative estimates. Come with me. Help me, and lie for me, and you will return to Sparrow Court as its true lady in five years."

"And if I refuse? Am I to be returned to Wilda?"

Ever sighed. "No, lady. You will not be returned to Sparrow Court unless you ask for it. I am asking for your help to be given freely."

I considered him, trying to work out in my mind how he could be tricking me, but I could not find his deception. "If I agree to this, what do you require of me? What will I do each day?"

"I require nothing of you but the single lie. If you agree to my bargain, you'll have your own house, your own staff— you'll live a life of leisure. You don't have to see me at all, except for the few events I am required to attend at the palace, which will require my wife at my side. Other than that, your life will be completely your own."

I nodded. "And if I wanted to work? Would you allow that?"

"I can assist in establishing contact via letters to your Sparrow Court staff so you may oversee court in writing, but you don't need my permission—"

"No— I would appreciate that help, thank you— but I mean that I need something to do. Wilda has not allowed me to work, except as a companion and dresser to her daughters, for the past decade. I want to spend my time on something more pressing than braiding my stepsisters' hair," I explained. I held out my hand to shake his. "I will lie for you. I will tell the world that our marriage is sealed with our Soulbinding, if in exchange you give me a working estate to manage as your lady."

Ever stared at my outstretched hand, thinking my words over. I almost thought he would deny me, but he did the opposite and grasped my hand tightly. Ancient magic seemed to warm my bones when he answered, "It's a bargain."

An hour later we were on the road to Ever's house. He had promised it wouldn't be far, and that we would arrive by lunch time. True to his word, before the sun reached its highest point in the sky, we were pulling up to the front of a large vine-covered cottage in the center of a clearing surrounded by forest on all sides.

"It's nothing extravagant," Ever explained while I looked out the carriage window. "It seemed wasteful to live at one of the bigger properties when it's just me."

"It's pretty," I told him.

"Your place will be bigger," he promised. "The grounds of my other estates have plenty of room."

"I'm not worried about the size of it, Ever. Thank you— I can't begin to thank you enough for all of this."

"It's nothing compared to what you're doing for me, truly—" Ever cut himself off when a faerie came strolling out of his house. She had a look on her face somewhere between worry and anger when she stopped, crossing her arms over her chest while she stood in the front garden and waited. "Could you wait here for a moment?"

"Of course."

He left the carriage and approached the faerie. She dipped her chin in greeting, but I could not hear him when he started talking. He seemed to be explaining something— explaining *me*, I was certain. She glanced at the carriage, then back at him, with her eyebrows raised. Suddenly a horrible thought crossed my mind, and I found myself praying to any gods who would hear me that this faerie was not Ever's lover.

They spoke back and forth for another moment before Ever returned to the carriage and opened the door. "Thank you for waiting. Will you join us?" I accepted his offered hand as I took the few steps to the ground. The faerie stood expectantly; arms still crossed as she watched us approach. "Margot, this is Onyx of Nightfall, my aunt." I hoped neither of them heard the sigh of relief that escaped me. "Onyx, meet Margaret Brightwood, Lady of Sparrows. My wife."

"Friends call me Margot," I said, extending my hand to shake hers. Onyx looked at it, then back at my face before dipping her chin.

"Lady Margaret."

Slowly, I took my hand back, and we stood in uncomfortable silence.

"Margot," Ever started. "Onyx is aware of our arrangement and will be helping me to find a suitable place for you. Until then, my home is yours."

"Thank you," I said. "I'm sure I will be content."

Rhea came outside before Ever or Onyx could say anything else. "Oh good, you've made it." She kissed Ever's cheeks when she reached him, then turned and did the same to me. I was a bit stunned by her familiarity, but Ever did not seem to mind. "You must be starved."

"Oh, I ate breakfast just a couple of hours ago, but thank you."

"There's no use," Ever said. "Rhea will feed you if she deems it necessary. Why don't you let her show you to your room while Onyx catches me up on what I've missed the last few days?"

"That sounds nice," I agreed. He placed his hand casually on the small of my back, only for Rhea's benefit.

"I'll see you at dinner," he said. "Get some rest."

Rhea had prepared my room to perfection. It was smaller than my bedroom at Sparrow Court, but brighter. It was pretty and thoughtfully decorated in anticipation of its new occupant. Crisp, white sheets and a thick quilt the same amethyst color as my wedding dress hugged the mattress sitting on an oak frame. Across from the bed was a matching vanity, wardrobe, and writing desk. The floorboards were covered by a plush white rug that I imagined I would be quite thankful for if I were here when colder days came.

"The wardrobe has a few things in it for you," Rhea said. "And the bathroom is stocked with anything you might need. I will see to it that the rest of your belongings are there before you wake tomorrow. My lord's tailor will have to make a trip out to see you when you're more settled."

"That's not necessary—"

"Do you expect that your stepmother will send a trousseau?"

"...no."

"Then you will need some new things," Rhea said. "My lord thought you might protest. He said the cost is of no concern. You are the Lady of Sparrows and of the Waterways. You cannot be limited to only a handful of aged dresses."

"I suppose you're right," I said. The humiliating reminder that I had no money washed over me. At least in Sparrow Court it was my own money that I was dependent on Wilda for. It was my money that supported her and my stepsisters. But here, having nothing, and being completely dependent on Ever was something that would take some getting used to.

Rhea showed me the other attributes of the room— how to lock the vanity drawer, where to locate the bell I could ring to call her, and the door that separated my and Ever's bedrooms. "It locks from your side, my lady." Rhea pointed out a bolt at the top of the door. "Soulbound couples hardly keep the door closed, but I imagine sometimes you'll need your sleep." She shrugged a little, and I noticed a dreamy smile on her face. "That's all there is to it, I suppose. I'll leave you to rest, my lady."

She left, and for the first time since I agreed to our deal, I was alone. There was no going back now, but I couldn't help but wonder what I'd gotten myself into.

7

The day passed by while I let myself be thoroughly lazy. A plate was delivered for lunch and I grazed on its contents while lying in bed, until I was so full and tired I couldn't keep my eyes open. I dozed in and out of sleep for a few hours, and when I eventually noticed the time, I forced myself to get out of bed and prepare for dinner.

When Rhea delivered me to the dining room, Ever was already waiting, standing with his hands behind his back. We greeted each other warmly, if a bit awkwardly, and if Rhea was not convinced she said nothing of it. When she left us, Ever pulled my chair out for me and as soon as we both were seated, plates of food appeared before us.

"Did you get some rest?" he asked before sipping on his wine.

"I did, thank you. I'm feeling quite well."

"Good." A pause, and then Ever added, "I've found you a house."

"Oh," I said with surprise. "So soon?'

He nodded, chewing. When he swallowed, he explained, "I only have a few besides this one. I'm sending you to the Darkwater Estate. It's not too far from here and fits all your criteria. I'm hiring your staff tomorrow morning. They'll arrive in the evening to prepare the manor, and the following day I'll deliver you to them."

I dabbed the corner of my mouth with a napkin. "That is quite fast."

"I know," Ever said. "I'm sorry to move you around so suddenly, but it looks like I'll be very busy in the coming weeks, and I don't want you sitting around waiting for me. I doubt I'll have another window of free time until the solstice."

"I see," I told him. "I'm sure with your work not being limited to a single court, you find yourself spread thin."

"Indeed. My work takes me all around Daybreak. I'm hardly ever home."

"Why live in Serpent Court then?" I asked. "Wouldn't Stag Court call for less travel on your part?"

"I'm not fond of life in Stag Court," Ever explained. "And Prince Orist likes to keep me close."

"Your father is very demanding of your time," I observed. Ever's brow furrowed.

"Prince Orist has his reasons for his demands. My opinions on their value does not change the fact that I am required to comply with them."

Ever's rank as a lord within Serpent Court would mean that he is compelled to follow the governing lord's commands, the same way Sparrow Court nobility would be compelled to follow mine whenever I returned home. The Lord of Serpents lived but did not govern his own court. Today, and every day for the last three hundred years, the Lord of Serpents lay in his bed in an enchanted sleep. During a fight with the King of Nightfall, both faeries had suffered the same fate at the hands of a misfired spell, and now they both had a succession stuck in limbo. The Lord of Serpents had no living heirs, so the decision was made that one of the High King's children would watch over the eastern court until the enchantment could someday be lifted. Orist was the youngest and had no other titles or lands he was responsible for, and so it was him who had ruled over Serpent Court these past centuries. The heir to the throne in Nightfall ruled as regent in his father's stead, along with a council made up of others in the line of succession.

"Is your bedroom to your liking?" Ever asked, changing the subject and snapping me out of my trailing thoughts.

"Oh yes, it's lovely. Thank you," I said. "It was comfortable. Easy to rest in."

"Good," Ever replied. "I cannot imagine your stepmother was one to allow for proper rest."

I shrugged. "Yes and no. I was not allowed to do any real work. Chores, or anything worthwhile to the court's function were forbidden, I assume for fear I would be able to convince workers to plot against her— not that any of them would let me lift a finger anyway. If I was caught doing nothing too near to her, I was made to act as my stepsisters' dresser. I tried my best to simply stay out of sight and remove myself as a target."

Ever made a face. "I cannot believe she made you dress them, after all else they did to you."

"I became quite good at doing Gwenna's hair," I joked over my embarrassment. "If anyone here needs me, I am at your service."

"I'll be sure to let Onyx know." Ever smirked.

"Let me know what?" Onyx practically glided into the room. She was stunning and severe, with tanned skin and sharp features like Ever. Her sheet of sleek, moonbeam-silver hair was cut to her chin with perfect precision, and her nearly black eyes bore into me in a way that equally fascinated and terrified me. I had never met a faerie from the mountainous neighboring kingdom, which, despite the barriers between our nations being lifted decades ago, held on to such secrecy. Rumor had it, some of the fae from Nightfall could turn into ravens, their sigil, on command. Some thought you must whisper a correct password while stepping over the border into Nightfall, or risk your own demise. And as a child, I'd been told by older children at court that to reach the border to begin with, one must pass through the forest where the ghost of Queen Aven wandered looking for souls to steal.

"We were just discussing Margot's many talents," Ever said, jolting me from my thoughts. I nearly scoffed. "And I've informed her of the decision to give her the Darkwater Estate."

"Won't you join us?" I asked, gesturing to an empty seat.

"I'm fine, thank you." She sniffed. "I'm off to bed," she said, turning away from me to face Ever. "I'll be gone before dawn to arrange for the sentries."

"That is fine, Onyx, thank you."

"Thank you," I repeated, perhaps too eagerly. "I appreciate your attention to this, Lady Onyx."

She dipped her chin just briefly. "The faster we get you settled, the faster Ever can return to the business at hand." Onyx said nothing else before turning on her heel and leaving.

"Have I offended her?" I asked.

"No." Ever sighed and practically rolled his eyes. "Ignore her."

"I seem to be quite the disruption."

"Onyx acts as if the world will end if I deviate from my schedule for a few days. She is, truly, always like that. It's not worth worrying yourself."

"But I *have* disrupted you?" I asked directly. "Eating with me, going through this trouble—"

"The minor disruption to my plans is worth the benefit of our deal,"

Ever said plainly. His tone sounded irritated by my endless need for clarification.

"Sorry," I said.

"Don't be," he said flatly.

We finished our meal in relative silence. Onyx's mood hung over us, and every exchange after that felt awkward. When we finished eating, Ever informed me that he had more work to do before he retired for the night, and that he would see me in the morning. It wasn't necessarily an order to return to my bedroom, but it was a dismissal, no matter how polite. And what else was I going to do? We bid each other goodnight and I left him.

An hour later I lay staring at the ceiling in the dark bedroom. It had been a long day— one of the longest of my life. I fiddled with my wedding ring, and the reality of what I'd done set in. A lie, in exchange for freedom. A lie for a life outside Wilda's control. I was grateful for all Ever had done for me in the past couple of days. If it weren't for him, I'd be back in Sparrow Court, no better off than I was before traveling to Prince Orist's home, instead of lying in a plush bed in a private bedroom that had no risk of my stepsisters barging in without warning and making demands of me. I wished he had asked about the deal before I'd exchanged blood with him, but then again there had not exactly been a chance. I knew, ultimately, that this was my best shot at a future for my court— and for myself. But gods, did I feel reckless for it.

My mind raced like that for another twenty minutes or so before I gave up on trying to sleep and decided to find something to read. There was nothing on the shelves in this room, but I remembered Rhea mentioning a study down the hall, where I imagined something helpful might be. I knew which door to go to and saw that it was cracked open. I heard Ever and Onyx's voices as I approached but couldn't make out what they were saying. They were clearly busy, so I turned around to head back to my room.

"Is everything alright, Margot?" Ever's voice called out from behind me. I grimaced and turned back to the door before pushing it open all the way.

"I'm fine, thank you." My face was pink with embarrassment. "I didn't mean to interrupt. I'll just head back to my room—"

"Was there something you needed?" Ever asked.

"I was searching for something to read. Sleep trouble."

"Ah," he said. "By all means, help yourself. You'll likely be inclined to the topmost shelf. Wouldn't want you to suffer through the stuffed-up lords you'll find on the others." His sarcasm had me stifling a laugh as I selected a small volume on beekeeping.

"This will do nicely. Thank you, Ever. Goodnight to you both."

"Sleep well, Margot."

8

The next day I slept late enough that I felt groggy and sore instead of rested. Rhea either heard or sensed my stirring somehow, and minutes after I woke she came scurrying through the door with a tray of food and an offer to help me dress, which I declined.

"My lord has already left for the morning," she informed me. "He asked that I tell you he will join you for dinner."

"When should I expect Lady Onyx to return?"

"Oh, by midday, I expect. She was off before sunrise."

"Oh," I said. I busied myself with making a cup of tea. I was happy to find today's brew was not stale.

"You must forgive Lady Onyx's manners," Rhea said gently. "She is quite loyal to my lord. If she is standoffish, I am sure it is just a matter of adjusting."

"Of course," I said a little dismissively. "Thank you, Rhea."

She seemed to take the hint and dipped her chin before mumbling her goodbyes and leaving as quickly as she had arrived.

I took my time bathing and dressing, and a few hours later I found a spot to read outside. I continued with the beekeeping book from the night before and took notes on a piece of stationary I brought along. These notes would all be sent to Mr. Dewstone, the steward of the palace in Sparrow Court, once I'd established contact with him. Our honey and especially our mead was once sought after throughout all of Daybreak. Besides use in its pure form, honey was used in everything from medicine and cosmetics to bread and cheese. Wilda had stopped its production in favor of the pursuit of dyeing textiles. Her plans included ripping up the acres of flowers that had attracted the bees season after season for centuries and planting new, more richly pigmented variations that were not suited to our climate. The crops failed and our hives relocated, causing a panic for the merchants when trade all but halted. My first order of business would be to invite the hives back. It would take several seasons to restore all the proper flower fields and the apiary to what they once were, but the result would be worth it.

I was so lost in my thoughts and planning that I did not notice anyone approaching until a shadow fell over my page as I wrote. I looked up and found Onyx standing over me.

"Hello," I said as warmly as I could muster.

"Hello, Lady Margaret," she said stiffly. "I do not mean to interrupt you for long. I only wish to inform you that your sentries have been hired. They are on their way to Darkwater now and will remain there until the last harvest. It will just be you and your house staff through the winter and the sentries will return to you in the spring."

I nodded. "That all sounds fine. Thank you for your help."

"It will be good for you to settle into Darkwater quickly," Onyx said. "It makes your farce easier to maintain if you and Ever are not in the same house."

"I'm sure it will."

"Ever's work is important," Onyx continued. "He needs as few distractions as possible. Orist knows this, which is why the marriage was ordered. There is enough sabotage of Ever's plans without there being a constant need for him to step away and check on the state of Darkwater. Do you understand what I am saying to you?"

"You're saying that I need to shut up and not make myself a problem," I said flatly. "I understand."

Onyx did not say another word before strolling back toward the house, leaving me fuming.

At dinner, Ever informed me of the three full time members of staff that would be living in the manor at Darkwater with me: a cook, a maid, and a steward to oversee everything else. The sentries and other grounds staff would have their own quarters and would be managed by the steward as well.

"They'll all be there to meet you tomorrow," Ever said.

"Perfect," I replied. "Thank you." I tried to seem uninterested. This dinner was an obligation with me as his house guest. Onyx made it clear that Ever had better things to do than entertain me. I was a distraction.

"Is everything alright?"

"I'm afraid I'm rather tired," I lied, picking at my food. "I think I may just go to bed, if you'll excuse me."

"Of course, Margot." Ever stood when I did, and I left him alone in the dining room.

The next morning, we made our way by carriage to the Darkwater Estate.

The road ran right up to a towering gate, and behind it my new sentries greeted me. There were ten of them, though only five would be on duty at any given time, so I would have guards day and night while they were present at the estate. This seemed like overkill to me, but Ever explained that there had been whispers of bandits growing active in the area, and if word got out that Darkwater was occupied, someone might come looking.

The long drive ended in a circle where the carriage could turn around. The driver stopped, and I peered out the window at the large, gray stone manor. Ever and I had been mostly quiet, only exchanging polite small talk on the way here. "Ready?" he asked.

"I suppose so," I said. Ever stepped out first so he could offer me his hand while I descended the carriage steps.

A handsome faerie with cropped, chestnut-colored hair and a gray suit was waiting for us. He held his hands in front of him, folded politely as we approached.

"Greetings Milord," he said. "Milady." His accent sounded nothing like the folk I'd encountered so far in Serpent Court. He must be from the countryside up north, I thought.

"Margot, this is the new steward of Darkwater Estate, Mr. Cypress. Mr. Cypress, the mistress of this house— Margaret Brightwood, Lady of Sparrows."

"Greetings, Mr. Cypress," I said and reached my hand forward. He took it and kissed the back, though I'd intended a handshake.

"Welcome, Milady," Mr. Cypress said. "The staff has been working hard to prepare for your arrival."

"Not too hard, I hope." He looked at me strangely. "I'm only one person, Mr. Cypress."

"Indeed, Milady." He smiled tightly. "Nonetheless, we are ready for you."

"Would you like to see the grounds first, or the manor?" Ever asked me.

"The grounds, please."

"Of course." He looked at Mr. Cypress. "Lady Margaret's belongings will need to be sent to her rooms. Would you be so kind?"

"Of course, milord." Mr. Cypress bowed his head slightly before leaving us to approach the carriage and retrieve my trunk. Mr. Cypress tapped each item and then snapped his fingers. The bags disappeared.

We rounded the side of the manor and I nearly gasped at the sight of the sprawling green before me, complete with multiple workhouses and garden beds. Not far off was the edge of an inky black lake— the estate's namesake. On the shore, two pairs of workers were shifting huge basins.

"What is that?" I asked.

"Your new job," Ever said. I raised an eyebrow. "Well, overseeing it anyway. Come along, I'll show you."

He guided me toward the workers— three fae, one human— who stood back and greeted Ever and me when we approached. Ever greeted them all by name before introducing me and explaining that I would be overseeing their work from now on. I waited for someone to explain what it was they were doing when Ever turned and did exactly that:

"Darkwater is a salt lake," he said. "They're harvesting the salt. See?" He then rolled his sleeves to his elbows and demonstrated the use of the basins and the layer of fine mesh that lay in them to collect the remaining salt once the water evaporated. "It's nearly the end of the season," he said. "It gets too cold in the late autumn and through the winter for the water to do anything but sit there, so these fine gentlemen will return to their homes when the sentries do. But come spring they'll return and will be plenty busy again." We exchanged a few more pleasantries and I indicated my interest in learning more of their craft before moving on.

Ever pointed out the stables, which to my surprise held an actual, breathing horse. He would be tended to by the salt harvesters during the warm month, and Mr. Cypress would take over his care come winter. He was used to help haul the basins in the summer when harvests were large, but he was available for my use if I ever desired it. Sparrow Court had horses at the palace, but only because we had such high numbers of humans living and working on the grounds. Most fae did not bother, instead relying on ragweed horses that did not require so much maintenance. The patch of ragweed growing in the other pens told me that more steeds could be called upon if needed.

Next, we passed some workhouses, and Ever explained their function, but it was when we passed by an empty set of faemade beehives that I nearly stopped in my tracks. Darkwater had an empty apiary. A place for bees, a place to practice—

"Here," Ever said, opening a large door and revealing a set of dark steps. "Is a spare cellar. It's empty now but can be used for salt storage should you find yourself with a surplus. There is a smaller space attached the house for your kitchens to use–"

"May I have a hive?" I blurted suddenly. I could hardly pay attention to anything he said after seeing the empty apiary. He looked at me strangely. "Sorry," I muttered.

"No need," Ever replied stiffly. "This estate has never kept a hive, but I don't see why you couldn't start. I'll make an inquiry for some beekeepers to assist. There may be wild hives in the woods you could convince to live in the apiary."

"And if I wanted to use this cellar for Sparrow Court's betterment, would you object?"

Ever looked at me thoughtfully, like he understood immediately. "You're going to start making mead."

I nodded. "It would not be true Sparrow Court mead, of course— but if I had the chance to practice while I'm here in Darkwater and learn from mead makers who know my court's methods, perhaps… perhaps I'll be able to give better direction in my letters once I've established contact with my steward back home."

He seemed to consider for a moment and then said, "Do what you like. If there are any supplies you need, send for them with your accounts here."

"I will repay you," I promised.

"That will not be necessary," Ever said. I was about to argue, but he continued speaking. "May I ask, why mead?"

"Sparrow Court has produced mead and honey products for–"

"No, I understand why *you* are doing it," he clarified. "But no one has ever been able to tell me why Sparrow Court specifically places such a high value on it. Sparrows do not produce honey, and yet bees seem to be revered equally to your sigil. Mead production has made your court wealthy beyond measure, but there's more to it, I imagine."

"Oh, yes." Ever closed the cellar door and we began walking back toward the manor. "Do you know what sparrows and bees have in common?" Ever shook his head. "They remember. Sparrows are the keepers of truth," I said. "Or, that's how my father put it anyway. The old legends say they will always know who is truly worthy to hold power. If you are truly worthy, they will remember you, no matter how long you are away from them. If you are not worthy, they will forget they ever knew you. It is how we continue to live, after death– because of their memory. Sparrows know the true hearts of those they encounter. They are utterly sacred."

"And the bees?"

I smiled. "Bees remember their caretakers. They know their masters, just as the sparrows do, and their favor is a blessing. To share in their bounty is a sacred responsibility."

Ever seemed to absorb the information. "So the mead…"

"I'm getting there," I joked. "My father insisted on the long-winded version of this story too. Indulge me."

"Go ahead," he smirked.

"*Mead is a memory,*" I said, quoting Papa again. Ever looked confused. "I could take honey made from the prettiest summer wildflowers, or sweet lemon blossoms in the springtime, and turn it into a drink that freezes that moment forever. The second it touches your lips, you are taken back to the day, the season, the minute it was made. For as long as your goblet lasts, you are blessed with that memory. The bees give that to us. Between them and the sparrows, we can live forever in the hearts of those who will remember us too."

Ever's face was contemplative. "It's silly, I know–"

"It's not," he insisted. "That's a pretty story, Margot, thank you for sharing it with me."

We walked in silence the rest of the way to the house, where Ever led me on a tour of the main floor– entry, dining room, library, parlor, and kitchen– before taking me upstairs to view my suite at the end of a long hallway with four doors on each side. "Extra bedroom suites," he explained. "Not ready for guests just yet but can be made so quickly if necessary."

My suite was simple but large, nearly twice the size of my bedroom at Ever's house. My luggage sat neatly stacked in the center of the floor. There was an enormous bed, vanity, and wardrobe. On the other side was a fireplace, table and chairs which would seat four for private entertaining. Ever pointed out the bathroom through one door before leading me through another at the back of the suite, which led to a spacious study. An enormous desk carved from elm took up most of the space, the walls were lined with matching bookcases and a fireplace that sat cold behind the desk.

"Here we are," Ever said, as he walked to the desk and pulled out a chair for me to sit. I did, and he produced a thick book bound in red leather, and a thinner one in black. "This–" he gestured to the black book. "Is the ledger with all the details specific to Darkwater. The red contains the details of all my estates and merchant accounts. I have copies of both. There are spells on both our copies, so if either of us makes a note, it will reflect in the other ledgers and we will always be up to date. Go ahead and flip through it."

Hesitant, I opened the red book and began skimming the information. I felt my eyes go wide and I pulled it closer, as if I would better understand what I was seeing. "You're sure this is correct?"

"Down to the copper, yes."

I read the page again, drumming my fingers on the desk. "Ever," I breathed. "You— this is more money than I've ever seen. Sparrow Court doesn't even come close— not even when I was a girl." I closed the ledger and faced him. "There's... that has to be more than the *crown*."

"It's a close second," Ever said. "No one, especially not from the Stag Palace, can know the contents of those ledgers."

"Of course. Not exactly polite dinner conversation."

"I'm serious, Margot." His voice was stern. "I do not think it is a secret that I am not well liked at the palace. If anyone asks about our accounts, it is in the interest of your safety that you do not tell them. Show those ledgers to no one."

"Why did you show me, if it is so dangerous?"

"You wanted an estate to run," Ever said plainly. "You'll see in those records, salt production is very profitable. This is not some throw-away position, Margot. I am trusting you to oversee this."

"I understand," I said. "Thank you for trusting me, Ever. I will not let you down." Why he trusted me so easily, I had no idea. It was an honor, regardless. "Are there other dangers at this estate that I should prepare myself for?"

"Nothing that you should spend too much of your time worrying about." Ever slid his hands into his pockets. "Your sentries can handle any potential countryside bandits if that's what you're worried about. All the anti-Avenists stay up by the northern border." I laughed. I did not know much about the anti-Avenists, except that they argued against the current system set in place by the old Queen of Faerie. They believe that her magic could be bent or broken if enough powerful fae banded together, and that the current system only serves the noblefae, so those in power will not attempt to change it.

"And if a whole army of anti-Avenists descended upon Darkwater, what shall I do then?" I asked, smiling.

"Hope you're faster than them and make a break for the stables," Ever instructed, half-joking. "At full speed, you'd reach my house in less than an hour."

I scoffed and leaned back in my chair with my arms folded across my chest. "In that case, I hope you'll pick out a nice headstone for me. Any full-blooded faerie would catch me on foot in a heartbeat. I suppose I'll just have to place my trust in the sentries against all those terrible bandits."

Ever smirked. "You should. Onyx chose them, so if she was impressed, I trust her judgment. But here–" From nowhere, Ever produced a small white drawstring bag. It appeared to be filled with something–herbs, perhaps–and was tied tightly at the top. He squeezed it in his palm and it glowed brightly for a few seconds before he handed it to me. I looked at it, then at him, waiting for an explanation. "If it is a matter of life and death," he said. "Set this alight and the danger will be dealt with."

"How ominous," I noted before tucking the sachet away in the desk drawer. "Thank you for the peace of mind. I'm sure it won't be necessary." We fell quiet for a moment. Ever's hands returned to his pockets, and I made myself very interested in the top of the desk.

"Well," Ever said, breaking the silence. "I suppose there is nothing left to show you. You're in excellent hands with your staff."

"Oh, you're leaving..."

"I'm afraid so. Merchant meetings. Onyx is probably pacing my study, wearing a hole in the floor as we speak."

"I see." The thought of being here alone was suddenly terrifying. Of course, I'd known it was coming all along. That was the point of all of this. "I certainly would not want to keep you from your work."

"There is just one more thing," Ever said. I noted some hesitation in his voice.

"Oh?"

He cleared his throat. "Given our arrangement, I simply wanted to make it clear to you that I have no expectations of your... fidelity."

It took a few seconds for me to understand. I blushed. "Oh."

"Yes— I only ask for your discretion. It would give things away if you were too public with an affair." I nearly laughed. If only he knew how unlikely that was. I had tried to rid myself of my maidenhead plenty of times over the years, to no avail. I did not exactly have a line of suitors waiting. Now that I was married to Ever, I was sure my prospects had shrunk considerably.

"Of course," I told him. "Anything else?"

"Do your best not to bankrupt me," Ever said with a smirk. I smiled, and he added, "I cannot thank you enough, Margot."

"We both win here," I assured him.

"Yes, we do." He cleared his throat again. "I will see you by the solstice. Should you need anything before then, feel free to write."

"I will."

"Well then," Ever said. He took one of my hands in his own and kissed the back of it. "Lovely wife, I wish you an easy time getting settled."

"I'm sure I'll feel quite at home here, Ever, thank you."

"Good day, Margot." And then he was gone.

9

I spent the next few days settling in and forming a routine.

In the mornings, I would attend breakfast in the dining room where I felt quite silly eating alone at a table that could easily seat ten. Though I would feel even sillier taking meals in my room like a shut-in. Arlie, the housekeeper, woke me in the mornings and helped me dress for the day. She was not quite as small as the cleaning staff at Prince Orist's manor had been, but she had a similar scratchy, high-pitched voice, hairy, pointed ears, and long, sharp canines that sometimes poked past her lips even when her mouth was closed. After Arlie finished helping me start my day she insisted that she serve my meals, which were prepared by a dark-haired, towering human cook named Vic who I hardly saw unless I needed to pass through the kitchen for something. Even then, he was busy stirring pots on the stove or scrubbing them in the sink, as he provided not just my meals, but those of all the workers and sentries on the property. When I suggested I write Ever and request a second cook to help him, Vic took great offense and banned me from the kitchen altogether.

Mr. Cypress brought my mail to the table each morning. When I established contact with the steward of Sparrow Court, Mr. Dewstone, I had Mr. Cypress set his letters aside to be taken to my study and dealt with later. Anything else I permitted him to read aloud, per his own offer, while I ate my breakfast.

When I finished, I would settle into my study and respond to Mr. Dewstone's daily letter. We agreed that our correspondence should not be revealed to Wilda, and that our first order of business should be the restoration of the apiary. I informed him of my intentions to utilize the empty hives here in the meantime and asked him to send any books my father may have kept on the topic of mead making, so that I might get a bit of practice before the cold truly set in— if I could find a hive.

After lunchtime, I walked to the lake to say hello to the salt harvesters, see if there was anything they needed, and check on progress myself despite not quite knowing what I was looking for.

Adrien, the lone human, kept his head down and focused only on the work even if I was present, not acknowledging me beyond a polite nod. His hair was sandy-colored and his skin, even with the cool, gray autumn weather rolling in, was golden-brown from working at the lakeside through the summers. He usually worked with his husband, Magnus, a tall faerie with wild, jet-black hair and matching, curved horns coming out of his head. He was happy to chat anytime I stopped by, and kindly indulged my questions.

The other two fae, who Magnus told me were twins named Felix and Tobias, never spoke to me, and hardly lifted their eyes when I approached. They each had gills on their necks and smooth yet scaled green skin, like a snake. They were content to do their work without the mistress of the estate pestering them, but I still made a point to observe them and their work so I might know them better.

It was only after that, and passing by the gates to wave hello to the sentries, that I would allow myself to take pleasure in the messy work of cleaning out the bee boxes.

I was close enough to the forest's edge while I worked that I could feel the stares and hear the snickering of the local woodsprites. I shook my head, laughing to myself as they whisper-yelled at one another and argued with the pixies that joined in their observation of me. Where woodsprites roamed, pixies would follow closely. Their mischievous chatter was more discreet, and slightly sinister, but kept me from too much quiet.

I decided to do my bookkeeping weekly. The first week, when I was finished updating the ledgers, I wrote a brief letter to Ever. I detailed any information that might benefit him that would not fit into ledger margins and informed him all was well at Darkwater. No response came.

At the end of my second week at the estate, my day was put on hold when the tailor that Rhea mentioned finally arrived, and I was made to have measurements taken while looking at various fabrics and sketches. My morning work would have to be put off for the next day.

It was midday when Mr. Cypress came knocking. "Milady?"

"Yes, Mr. Cypress?"

"I am sorry to disturb, but there is some commotion near the apiary."

"Commotion?"

"Something with the woodsprites, milady— they're demanding to see you."

"To see *me*?" I asked.

"Yes, milady. They grow restless. I would not suggest a slow pace."

"Of course, Mr. Cypress. Thank you." He dipped his chin and left the room to allow me privacy. Once I was changed into one of my old dresses, I swept out of the room, passing Mr. Cypress in the hallway. "Come along," I called over my shoulder.

"Me, milady?"

"Yes, you," I said. "You speak the forest tongue, correct?"

"I do."

"Well, I do not," I said. "I will require your assistance, please."

"Of course, milady."

I hurried down the stairs with Mr. Cypress at my heels, walking swiftly to keep up with my pace. When we arrived, at least ten woodsprites were flitting around excitedly in the air. Their translucent wings caught the sunlight, throwing rainbows and pretty sparkles. It almost made up for their grumpy, pinched faces with horrible, beetle-like black eyes.

As I approached, they all began calling for me and pushing one another out of the way. They spoke over the top of one another, and I did not understand a word any of them said. Mr. Cypress stepped forward and spoke in the forest tongue. One of the woodsprites came forward and spoke in a gravelly voice.

"He says they've found what you seek," Mr. Cypress informed me.

"And what would that be?" I inquired. He asked a question and waited for the woodsprite's response. Mr. Cypress looked puzzled. "What is it?"

"A strange translation on my part," he admitted. "I know the words he's saying but I fear I need more context. He just keeps saying what I know to mean *sugar house*."

"Can he show me?"

"It would not be wise for you to follow the woodsprites into the forest, milady."

"Will you ask, please?"

Mr. Cypress said something else to the woodsprites and they all got excited again, taking off into the tree line. I followed swiftly, keeping my eyes on the creatures in front of me. I knew better than to let my gaze wander in unfamiliar woods, despite the authority I held here. As the trees grew denser and the light dwindled, I heard Mr. Cypress say behind me, "Milady, I don't know that this is the best choice."

"I am not afraid, Mr. Cypress."

"I understand, but there is more hiding in the forest than pixies and woodsprites."

"They want to help." I shrugged. "And I would like to know what they're talking about."

"Yes, but are they helping you or something else—"

"Are you coming, Mr. Cypress?" I asked as I cut him off while continuing forward. There was silence behind me for a moment followed by the continued sounds of trudging through the brush. I smiled to myself at the thought of Mr. Cypress' exasperation.

We followed the woodsprites for another few minutes, being led over loose rocks and fallen trees that slipped under my shoes and snagged my skirts. More than once, Mr. Cypress had to catch me under my elbow to keep me from hitting the ground. I heard him mumble to himself about the frivolous clothes of noblefae and their impracticality. I could feel his nerves bubbling as we trekked deeper into the dark trees.

"They say we're here," Mr. Cypress informed me as the woodsprites erupted into excited chatter again. The pixies followed too but did not speak as they observed us from high in the branches, their yellow-green eyes flashing in the dark. The woodsprites zipped along, leading me into a bright clearing, and the sounds of crunching branches were replaced with loud buzzing in my ears.

An enormous, beautiful beehive was wedged in the branches of a tree across the clearing, nearly glowing and golden in the noontime sunlight.

"My gods," I breathed.

"*Sugar house,*" Mr. Cypress said, shaking his head. "I should have guessed."

I turned and faced the woodsprite that seemed to be leading the rest of them. "What is your name?" Mr. Cypress repeated the question and the woodsprite responded.

"He says it's Sunn."

"Sunn, you have done me a great kindness."

"He says: Mistress needed bees. Mistress will give honey to Sunn."

"Ah," I chuckled. "That seems a fair payment for your assistance. I shall be sure that you receive a share of the honey each month, should the Queen decide to stay with us." Mr. Cypress repeated my message. Sunn and the other woodsprites cheered.

"They are pleased, milady."

"As am I. Good day to you, Sunn." The woodsprites took off into the trees, speaking excitedly while I set my sights on the hive.

"Milady, was that perhaps a bit reckless?" Mr. Cypress asked as we both approached the hive.

"What was reckless?" I removed my shoes and began gathering the edge of my skirts in my hand so I would not trip on them. Mr. Cypress averted his eyes to the ground.

"Making deals with the woodsprites. They can be quite vicious when crossed."

"I do not plan on crossing them, so I fail to see the problem."

"Do you truly intend to gift them your crops—"

"It is repayment for a service, Mr. Cypress, and it is more than fair. Darkwater can manage a single jar of honey to the woodsprites each month." I began climbing up the tree. "We have woodsprites in Sparrow Court, you know. I can manage."

"I do not doubt that milady, it is just unusual for someone in your position to make dealings with lesser folk."

I rolled my eyes and kept climbing. *Lesser folk* was a term I'd only heard a few times, to describe fae creatures like pixies, woodsprites, hobgoblins, and the like. The same fae who thought themselves better than them could typically be counted upon to have cruel opinions of humans too. "You would do well to keep your opinions of who is 'lesser' to yourself, Mr. Cypress," I told him bluntly. "We are all fae, just the same. If you cannot bring yourself to work for someone who shows basic decency to those who help her, I am happy to relieve you of your position."

Mr. Cypress blanched and stammered something about slips of the tongue and not meaning any offense, but I had already turned my attention to the hive that I now shared a branch with. I steadied my breath and began speaking in soft tones, addressing the queen:

"Greetings, Your Majesty. I am the lady of these woods. If you feel so inclined, I wish to extend my invitation for you to take up residence near my house. It will be warmer there, come winter, and I only ask to share in your bounty. I will leave a trace to help you find your way.

Thank you." I climbed down and sat at the base of the tree to return my shoes to their feet.

"Shall I send for someone to transport this colony to your hives, Milady?"

"No, Mr. Cypress. The queen will lead her subjects to the apiary if she chooses to accept my offer," I said. I held up a discarded piece of comb to show him before slipping it into my pocket. "They'll follow the scent and find their honeycomb in the boxes. Stealing a hive is dreadful luck."

"Oh," he said. "I was not aware it was considered theft."

"Tell that to the bees," I replied. I began trudging back the way we came, leaving Mr. Cypress to follow at his own pace.

That night I wrote my second letter to Ever since arriving at Darkwater. It gave a summary of the week's production, with a few notes about my personal projects with the apiary. I inquired as to whether he had any experience in handling the inhabitants of the woods and if I should expect any negative results from my agreement with the woodsprites. I sealed the page with wax and asked Arlie to have it sent out the following morning. I hoped, perhaps foolishly, that I might have his response to my first message by then.

Though Ever's silence hung over me, I kept writing my letters. The third detailed my surprise to find the apiary occupied, and the fourth informed him that the beekeepers he hired to assist me in the hives' care had arrived.

Despite awkward beginnings, Mr. Cypress was a dutiful steward. He and Arlie were vital while I got a grasp on my duties. Arlie would assist in my dressing and made sure I ate when I found myself buried in my work and stuck in my study for hours on end. She took my outgoing letters for me, but it was Mr. Cypress who still read my incoming letters to me at the breakfast table; a little ritual that I quite enjoyed.

Mr. Cypress in particular I found to be helpful and charming, though I also caught moments of snark that perhaps I wasn't supposed to see. When discussing the need for a winter wardrobe with Arlie, I could have sworn I saw him roll his eyes. I noticed him mumbling under his breath when handling the silver or other valuables in the house as well. He never did it if he knew I was watching, but I'd caught him enough times now that I became self-conscious. It was too much. Of course, on some level, I had always known that. I was raised in a palace, I was not unaware of my wealth, or of Ever's, but I'd never seen anyone's disdain for it up close. I noted in my ledgers that I was giving my staff a hefty raise. I was truly the least I could do. They were keeping a nine-bedroom manor up and running for just me, without any expectation of my favor. I wished, privately, that I would soon win theirs. They were, of course, dreadfully polite— but sterile. They were not friendly. We were not friends. Aside from the polite exchanges and basic requests, I could go most of the day without speaking to anyone.

A month after the forest hive moved into the apiary, though we were well into autumn, I received word from the beekeepers that there was enough honey for a small harvest. Giddy with excitement, I practically ran down to assist them. Arlie's eyes widened when she saw me leave the house in gardening trousers. The beekeepers seemed impressed by my knowledge of what they were doing and amused by my insistence that I help them.

This small harvest would likely be our only one until the summer. The bees would need to make enough to last them through the winter, and with the size of this hive, if there was extra, it would not be much. Regardless, I thanked their queen profusely and the beekeepers promised they would alert me if they noticed any overproduction that could be used as a rare late-autumn harvest. We set aside the honey for the mead makers who would come the next day, and I took two small jars back to the house with me.

With my letter to Ever that week, I packaged a small bounty from my kingdom of honey and salt: one of the jars of honey alongside a small container of the latest salt harvest. The other jar of honey would go to Sunn and the woodsprites. Mr. Cypress was in the study with me, dropping off a late letter from Mr. Dewstone, when I called Arlie in to take the package. When she left, I said mostly to myself, "I wonder if he'll like it." The words were sadder than I'd meant them to be.

"I fail to see how he would not, Milady."

"Perhaps I'm overstepping," I said. "He's obviously busy."

"Milady, it is a kindness. Your husband, forgive me, would be a fool not to see that. I am sure he can spare a moment to respond to you soon."

"I just want him to know this estate is in good hands."

Mr. Cypress' expression softened. "I'm sure he knows that, milady."

It was two days before I received a response. I was at the breakfast table, picking at eggs and toast that I didn't particularly want, when Mr. Cypress arrived with the mail tray. As usual he began opening the wax seals of each envelope and reading the contents:

"Two letters from Sparrow Court today, Milady," he said. "The first is from Mr. Dewstone."

"Have it sent to the study, please, I'll take a look at it later."

"The next is from your stepsister, Giselle," he said. I furrowed my brow. Neither she, nor her mother or sister were supposed to know where I was. He scanned the lines quickly. "She says she sent the same letter to all of Lord Oakshadow's known properties, hoping you will receive one..." He trailed off, reading silently, and then coughed to hide a snorting laugh. "She says you are needed at Sparrow Court at once, as her servants do not do her hair properly, and she requires your help in teaching them."

I scoffed before taking a deep drink of my tea. When I swallowed, I said, "Throw it away."

"As you wish ma'am." Mr. Cypress said with a hint of a smile. When he unfolded the next letter and began reading, that smile quickly disappeared. He turned the letter over to look at the broken wax.

"What is it?" I asked, noticing his concern.

"The next letter bears Lord Oakshadow's seal, milady."

"What does it say?" I asked nervously. He hesitated. "Mr. Cypress, please. Read the page for me."

Mr. Cypress sighed. *"My Lady, I thank you for the package, and for your detailed reports these last weeks. Please save yourself the trouble of writing them in the future, as I do not have need of such correspondence. Best Wishes."* My steward looked pained as he folded the page again and set it aside. I couldn't bear his pity.

"Well," I said, feeling my face grow hot. "I suppose that saves some time in my weeks now, doesn't it?" I stood from the table, plucking the napkin from my lap and laying it over my plate. "I think I'll change and go for a walk."

"It's going to rain, milady."

"I won't melt," I said.

I must have traced the perimeter of the grounds three times. As the clouds rolled in, dark and heavy, I found myself beside the lake, staring across the smooth surface of the inky water that only now began to ripple with the wind. I waded into the lake up to my knees, with a trouser pocket full of flat stones I found along the water line during my walk. It was only here, now, that I began to cry softly while I skipped the stones across the surface of the water.

Gods, I was lonely.

At least back at Sparrow Court my stepsisters spoke to me, even if it was only to tell me what I'd done wrong or to order me around. The other fae there treated me with kindness. I'd known them my whole life. Here, I was little more than a fixture. No companions, just silent staff moving around me as they did their work. Just them in their world and me in mine, quietly observing them. Little more than a stranger, watching from the outside.

When the rain finally did start, I continued my skipping. When I ran out of rocks, I bent down to find more in the mud, soaking my shirt front as I dirtied my palms and bloodied my fingernails in a blind search.

"Milady?" I heard a shout from the edge of the lake. I ignored it and kept going. "Milady, you will catch cold if you remain—"

"Leave me."

"Milady, I cannot." I glanced over my shoulder. Mr. Cypress was drenched from the rain.

"I said go," I told him. "I want to be alone."

"No, you don't."

"You don't know what I want," I yelled over the wind.

"Perhaps we should discuss this inside before you fall ill." I ignored him and continued throwing rocks. They weren't skipping anymore. "Milady, I will have to come in there and get you."

I whipped around. "You'll do no such thing, Mr. Cypress," I snarled. He began walking toward me anyway. "Leave me," I told him again. He was right in front of me. "I said—" He scooped my body into his arms before carrying me out of the water. I was kicking at him all the while. He marched us back to the manor, stoic, as I yelled at him. *"When my husband hears of this—"*

"Your husband is the reason for your anguish, milady. You'll fall ill if you remain in the water—"

"Then let me," I said in quiet defeat.

"I cannot do that." There was that pity again. His voice dripped with it. "Let's get you warmed up."

Mr. Cypress carried me to my bedroom and summoned Arlie before stepping out to allow me some privacy. Soon enough, I was changed and sitting before the fireplace with a blanket and a steaming cup of strong tea, to which Mr. Cypress added a splash of something stronger from a flask he pulled out of his inner coat pocket.

"Are you feeling better?" he asked.

"I would feel better," I said, setting the cup and saucer on the table beside me. "If I were more than a prisoner in my own home."

"You are not a prisoner, milady," Mr. Cypress assured me. "You are not trapped. You may go wherever you like—"

"My husband put me here nearly two months ago and has not looked upon me since. You read the message yourself. Lord Oakshadow does not wish to communicate with me in any form."

The steward frowned and folded his hands in front of him. "I'm sure your lord husband has his reasons for his absence. If it is any consolation, it is little more than a month until the solstice, and—"

"And I will be collected to sit prettily beside him and hold his arm and say nothing, only to be dumped back here to succumb to my loneliness when he's through with me."

"Are you lonely, lady?"

"How could I not be?" I asked, and my voice cracked. "This conversation is the first time you or anyone in this house has spoken to me like a person." I slumped in my seat and retrieved my cup from the saucer once again. "It would be nice, occasionally, to be reminded that I exist. It's easy to forget whether I'm a real person or not."

"You are very real, milady," Mr. Cypress said kindly.

"What is your first name?" I asked suddenly.

He hesitated half a second, then told me, "It's Reed."

"Reed," I repeated. "I would like it if we got to know one another better."

"You would?"

"Yes. We live in the same house, after all. Would you care to join me for a cup of tea?"

"Milady—"

"—Margot."

"Margot." Reed sighed, hesitating. "You flatter me, but I cannot join you tonight."

"Oh." I flushed. "Oh, of course. I'm sorry—"

"You misunderstand, Mil— Margot." He dropped his voice lower. "It's not because I don't want to, it's just... the walls in this house have ears. You, alone with a male member of your staff in your private quarters, after I've just carried you up here... it would be deemed improper."

"Oh... yes, of course. I wasn't thinking."

"You were kind to invite me." He flashed a tight smile. "And you are kind to want to know me better. Perhaps, sometime when I am free of my duties for the day, I can escort you to the hives."

"You would do that?" I asked.

"Of course," Reed replied. We both paused awkwardly, and after a minute or so he added, "I had better leave you to your evening, milady. Arlie will bring your dinner in an hour or two. If you require anything further, do not hesitate to ask us."

"Thank you, Reed. For everything." He bowed his head again and left without another word.

10

As promised, two days later when I went to visit the beekeepers, Reed met me at the door.

All our interactions since he carried me out of the lake were brief, but gentle. He asked me about my day, about what book I was reading, or what my evening plans were. Simple questions, nothing too pressing or personal for the mistress of Darkwater, but just enough to show that he noticed me— and gods, what a nice feeling, to be noticed. As small of a gesture as it was, it was just enough to have me looking at him in a different light.

Reed looked rather dashing when he offered me his arm, and I blushed, feeling silly. He was being polite, and regardless, I was his employer. Or my husband was. Finding him attractive was inappropriate. Even if the sunlight caught beautifully in his chestnut hair when it curled around the points of his ears. Even if his sharp jaw created the perfect frame to his face.

Even if he had waded into the muck to ensure my safety during that last storm.

I shook the thoughts away when we arrived, and I began my inspection of the hives. Reed did not say much or ask what I was doing when I peered inside to see how much the colony was slowing. I knew they would soon form their cluster to keep warm during the winter months, and I was still holding out hope for one more late harvest, even if it was small. I was discussing this with the beekeepers for a few moments and reminded them to keep me updated if and when there was enough, before moving on to the mead cellar.

Reed hoisted the door open, and I took his offered hand while descending the steps into the darkened room. He stayed at the top while I checked the progress on the glass jugs prepared by the mead makers, noting the foamy bubbles forming in each one. Excitement fluttered in my chest, followed by a flash of grief that Papa was not here to see me doing this. I blinked away a couple of tears before returning to the daylight.

"How is it?" Reed asked.

"Great," I said. "It's drinkable now, but it's best if it's left to sit until spring. Or later. We'll have to be patient."

"I can't wait to try it. Sparrow Court mead is legendary."

"Well, it won't be true Sparrow Court mead," I corrected. "That must be made within the western border. This is just practice."

"Even so," he said. "It will be a pleasure to try your creation. Perhaps I'll have the chance to taste the real thing one day."

"You've really never tasted it?"

Reed scoffed. "Even if it had been available, I've never once been able to afford it. I cannot think of anyone I know who has. Such luxuries aren't afforded to us lowly commoners." He turned his gaze away from me when he added, "Few things are, unfortunately."

"Oh." I wasn't sure what to say to that. I tried to lighten the mood. "If it makes you feel any better, I had not tasted my father's mead in a decade before my wedding. Ever made sure I received a glass during our feast."

"Did he really," Reed replied flatly. "How thoughtful." His tone was icy, and I could tell he did not think much of my husband.

"What did you do before you came to Darkwater?" I asked, changing the subject completely.

"Oh, a little bit of everything." Reed grinned slyly. "Some work with my brothers."

"You must miss them."

"Surely," he said. "But I find my position to be quite appealing."

"Do you?"

"I'm quite content with my prospects here at Darkwater. I like working for you, Margot." I blushed. That was the first time he called me Margot unprompted.

We looked away from one another, and without another word I held on to Reed's arm while he guided me back to the house.

Over the following weeks, Reed and I began to spend even more time together.

He began delegating tasks to Arlie that he usually insisted on seeing to himself, in order to be at my side at nearly all hours of the day.

One day, I received word that the beekeepers would be able to manage one last harvest after all, and we rushed to the apiary so I could assist them myself. Without much excess, it was delicate work. With no time to waste, we hurried the fresh honey to the cellars, where the mead makers were waiting. I had asked Arlie to send word to them so they would be ready to work right away.

I watched nervously as they bottled everything up— without use of their magic, the way it was done at home— and set it on the shelves to age and ferment in the dark. Three more gallons. It would make about a dozen more bottles. A dozen more chances to improve my court.

"Are you alright?" Reed asked. He was standing beside me today rather than waiting outside. He always seemed to keep himself in arms' reach now. I realized I was shaking.

"Yes," I half-lied. "I'm just a bit nervous."

"About what?" he asked. "You got your harvest. More on the shelf, more gold in the Sparrow Court vault." That last comment dripped in sarcasm.

"Maybe," I agreed. "But only if I manage not to mess it up somehow."

"I do not think you messed it up. You've hired mead makers who know Sparrow Court methods. Beyond that, I don't know how else you think this should work."

"You're right," I said and faced Reed. "I'm just worried that... Oh, nevermind. I'm being stupid."

"Try me."

"My father was respected," I said. "Fae all over Daybreak, anytime he is mentioned, tell me how much they loved him. They tell me about how well he took care of his people, and all the things he achieved as a fair, just, governing lord. I worry that I cannot achieve the same. Now that I have my position back— or nearly so— I must start leading, sooner rather than later. The mead is the start of that."

"... is the mead some sort of metaphor?"

"No, the mead is just the mead." I shrugged, then admitted: "Looking at what I've started terrifies me. Sparrow Court was special, the things we made were special because of Papa. They were rare, and worthy of reverence. What if I don't have it, whatever it was that made him so beloved?"

Reed did something he never had before, and hooked his knuckle under my chin, gently forcing me to look up at him instead of avoiding his gaze by staring at the dirt cellar floor. "I believe you are as worthy of your peoples' love and your seat of power in Sparrow Court as you are of your position here." Then, a second thing he'd never done before: Reed bent down to kiss me.

It was warm, and well done. When we parted, his face had lost all its color. "Margot— milady— I..."

"Reed," I said breathlessly. "I don't know what to say."

"That's— that's fine. If you want me to, I'll go pack. I'll send my resignation to Lord Ever myself. I am so, so—"

I gripped his collar and kissed him back.

When we parted again, he stared at me, bewildered. I did not quite know what I was doing, but he was so sweet, and so handsome. I had earned a little fun, hadn't I?

"What are we going to do about this?" he asked softly.

"Not sure," I breathed. "But I don't want it to stop if you don't." This time when his lips met mine, we were both expecting it. It was deeper, more urgent as his tongue slipped past my teeth and his arms wrapped around my waist, pulling me to him so my body was flush with his. Heat reached my cheeks and all the way to the points of my ears.

When we pulled away again, Reed said, "I can be anything you need me to be." And as the low afternoon sun became evening, I found myself losing the desire to be anywhere but here.

Reed and I did not speak of our encounter in the cellar for two days, though it was not for lack of trying. Just as I was so lonely only a few weeks before, I was suddenly aggravated by a seemingly constant audience. Arlie, Vic, or one of the sentries seemed to always be nearby. Reed kept up appearances well— I was the only one who noticed him staring at me from across every room we found ourselves in together. A strange sort of fire seemed to dance in his gaze, and I was happy enough to bask in its warmth. It felt like hunger, like he was waiting for the perfect moment to devour me.

We finally found ourselves alone in my study as I poured over ledgers, and Reed stole a greedy kiss.

"If I don't have a minute alone with you soon, I think I may go mad," I said.

"Patience, milady," he murmured against my mouth. "All will come in due time." He brushed his lips against mine once more just as Arlie returned with a fresh ink bottle to refill my pens.

That evening at dinnertime, I decided to take matters into my own hands. When I was finished, Arlie approached to take my plate while Reed began sifting through the afternoon's letters.

"Arlie," I said before she could turn to leave.

"Yes, milady?"

"What are your plans for this evening?" I asked.

"Plans? Oh, I was going to do a bit of my mending, milady, and go to sleep early. But if there is a task that requires my attention, I can certainly set the mending aside for another day."

"I have no task for you," I said. "But I do wonder if you might join me for cards in my suite."

"Y-you want... me?"

"To play cards, yes." I looked at Reed, who was staring at me strangely. "Mr. Cypress, would you care to join us?" He sighed, and I noticed the corner of his mouth quirk upward.

"Of course, milady."

An hour into our game, Arlie yawned, and lay down a pair of tens.

"You win again, Arlie," I declared. "That makes three hands in a row."

"I used to play with my sisters back home," Arlie grinned. Her pointed teeth glinted in the lamp light. "I beat them every time too."

"Perhaps another round will give Lady Margot or myself a taste of that luck," Reed suggested, shuffling the cards as he spoke.

"Oh, no, Mr. Cypress. Milady, my apologies, but I'm afraid I'm much too tired for another hand."

"That's alright, Arlie." I turned to Reed. "Mr. Cypress, should we attempt a practice round now that we stand a chance against one another?"

Reed played along. "I don't see why not."

"Goodnight milady. Mr. Cypress." Arlie left us, so tired that she did not take account of the fact that she was leaving me alone with Reed, at night, in my private quarters.

The door had barely clicked shut and Reed was practically pulling me into his lap. Each kiss had heat rushing to my cheeks, to the points of my ears. His hands ran down my back and brazenly gripped my backside before moving on to my legs. His fingers clenched at my thighs, bunching my skirts into his fist. Reed's kisses landed across my face, then down my neck, sucking at the sensitive flesh and making me dizzy.

"You've very good at this," I gasped.

He chuckled. "I know." He returned to sucking on my collarbone, a sensation so delectable my eyes closed, and a moan escaped my throat. Reed's laugh vibrated against my skin.

"Have you done this a lot?" I choked out.

"Not with my employers, no," Reed joked. "But then again none of them have ever looked like you."

"But— other fae?"

Reed removed his hands from my legs and pulled his face far enough away that he could look at mine fully. "Do you want to stop?"

"No," I insisted. "No, I just... am realizing suddenly that I have no idea what I'm doing."

"No idea? But you are Soulbound..."

My face felt bright red with heat as I repeated my lie. "Yes. It was... quick. And just the one time."

"We should stop." Reed slid me from his lap and into the chair beside him. Embarrassed, I held my face in my hands.

"I'm sorry," I said after a minute. "I don't know what's wrong with me. I was enjoying myself, really."

"It's your husband," he said.

"That's—"

"You are Soulbound, Margot. Hesitation with anyone but him is going to be part of it." Reed ran a hand through his hair. "Most Soulbound fae cannot stand to look at anyone else, regardless of how miserable their spouse might make them. I'm shocked that I'm able to hold your attention at all."

"I want to try this," I told him.

"I'm in no rush, Margot. You shouldn't be either." Reed's fingers traced my jawline before kissing me again. "It's probably best if I let you get some sleep anyway."

"You can stay," I suggested.

"I shouldn't," he said. "I'd love to, but we should practice discretion."

I nodded. He was right. I told him as much.

"I'll see you in the morning, then."

"Goodnight, sweet Margot."

11

After a night of reliving my thorough embarrassment, I decided I must do something about my struggles with Reed. I could not tell him the truth, and so I knew I must prepare myself for what would come eventually. I did not want to hold back with him any longer. I deserved some fun. I deserved this.

I ignored my duties for the day and decided to spend it in the library, finding some sort of information. I gathered a stack of texts designed to teach healers about the body, as well as a few romance novels like the ones Mama would read. I thought it best to be accurate before reading fiction, so I started with the healers' texts. An hour in, I tossed the volume aside with a sigh. Another explanation, another diagram explaining where each part was located and what its function was. All the information I'd known since before my first blood. Nothing here could tell me what it would all feel like.

To my left the stack of romance novels sat on a table. I hoped one of them would be better instruction for my impending love life. I scanned the titles— *Cloaked Lust, Knight of the Night, Smooth as Silk.* I snorted at the silly titles but finally picked one called *Burnt Skies* and began flipping through it. The story itself was not very exciting. However, it was only twenty pages in when the heroine and her betrothed began ripping each other's clothes off, and I no longer cared what else might happen in the plot. The author had been quite descriptive in their portrayal and soon, despite myself, I was squeezing my legs together in hope for some friction. The scene ended in only a few pages but it was at that point that I was happily reading the story, wanting more. Another hour or so passed before the heroine and the man who was traveling with her came upon an inn that only had one bed available and I grew excited once again. This time, I sat back, laying down the length of the sofa while my head rested on the arm. I tucked an overstuffed, beaded cushion behind me and began to devour the words.

Before I realized what I was doing, my hand had drifted down between my legs, rubbing in soft circles while the story carried on. I gathered my skirt in my hands and let it sit around my hips, exposing myself to the empty room while my fingers explored their surroundings. I softly brushed the wiry hairs and was surprised when I pushed just a little further and found that I was wet. The sensation jolted me, and soon, I lay the book aside, abandoning it completely while I continued dipping my fingers in and out, slipping across my apex in swift circles. I was panting and found myself gripping my breast over my bodice. I felt a flush rise in my face and my fingers pressed harder, faster while pressure rose along my spine. I was climbing up, up—

The door opened.

I froze.

Reed stepped inside and shut the door behind him before looking up and seeing me in my state of near undress.

Oh gods. This was it. I was going to die, here and now, of utter embarrassment. Reed did not recoil. The only sign of shock he displayed was the brief flare of his eyes. He licked his bottom lip before starting to walk toward me. Hastily, I tried to pull my skirt back down as he grew closer then sat in an armchair directly across from me.

"Don't stop on my account," he said.

"W-what?"

"Keep going." The quiet command was so bold that for a second, I was completely stunned. Reed did not break his stare while I did as he said. I lay back down, and dove in with my hand once again, this time over the fabric. I was not brave enough to expose myself that much just yet. I held Reed's stare while I worked in quickening circles, and the indecent sound of my panting and small moans filled the room. He remained silent as he stared, eyes fiery and hungry while his chin rested on his fist. I was climbing again, pressure rising. My eyes closed and my head fell back as I lost myself in pleasure— and then I felt something cover my working hand, adding more pressure and friction to the sensation. My eyes opened, and Reed was standing over me. His hand covered my own, and his face hovered just inches from mine. "Keep going," he said for the second time. "I want all you have to give." When he covered my mouth with his I cried out, having found my release at last. His hand kept working me through, until I was spent and squirming from the touch. Reed kissed me deeply again before pulling away and standing straight.

"Milady." He winked and said nothing else before turning and leaving me alone in the library, shutting the door soundly behind him.

We continued like this for weeks. Each day, Reed and I would go about our separate duties, playing our roles as lady and steward. Sometimes he would accompany me for various tasks and outings if I needed assistance at the hives or a translator when dealing with Sunn and the other woodsprites. At night, he would sneak to my chambers, and we would spend hours together. What started as drinking or playing cards would usually end with me in Reed's arms, kissing and breathing heavily, though we never went further than what we'd done that day in the library.

When the air turned truly icy and snow began sticking to the ground, the bees retreated to the hive and my work became scarce, only communicating with Mr. Dewstone every third day or so. Reed kept the estate running smoothly while keeping me entertained, suggesting books or games I could play on my own while he worked. The early winter days made him busier than ever now that we were trapped indoors. He complained that it was much easier to keep the estate clean when there was no one in it during the warmer months. The sentries left for the season, now that it was too icy to walk to and from the gates, and there was little chance of any threat being able to approach from the road, let alone make it to the house. The salt harvesters left, too. Magnus and Adrien went home to their village further south, near the Serpent Palace. Felix and Tobias did not bid me farewell or alert anyone that they were leaving. Magnus informed me that this was their routine every winter, and that they would return without word in the warmer months as well.

As the cold continued creeping in and the Solstice approached without word from Ever, I allowed myself to start planning for celebrations at Darkwater. It would just be Reed, Arlie, Vic, and myself but I thought it would be good to plan something. A shared meal at least. Reed made me promise I would not give him a gift, and I agreed, with the condition that he promise the same to me.

One night, Reed and I were playing cards in my suite as we usually did, and I expressed my desire to share a meal with all of them on Solstice night. Reed scoffed.

"What?"

"You're going to share your table with your servants? It isn't done, Margot."

"Perhaps not by your previous employers, but my father would often invite our staff to share our table for the solstices and equinoxes," I said. "They were family, they did a lot for us." Reed raised his eyebrows but didn't say anything. "I wish you wouldn't do that."

"Do what?"

"Act like I'm somehow being deceptive in telling you how we treated workers in Sparrow Court," I said, looking at my own cards now instead of him. "It is not my fault you were treated poorly in previous positions. I can only help how you are treated here. It seems you are committed to hating those who govern regardless of their character. The High King and the courts are not going anywhere. That magic was set in stone by Aven, it is not as if it can be changed."

"I know my history, thank you," he said snidely at my mention of Queen Aven. "I was raised with certain opinions about the nobility, yes. I'm afraid it has soured my opinion of most fae born into wealth."

"I see." I lay down a card. "And what should I do if I wanted to win your favor?"

"Funny that you assume you do not already have it." His lips quirked upward.

"I am Lady of Sparrows," I said. "I would imagine I'm at the top of your list of contempt."

"That spot is reserved for High King Edric." A pause. Reed was waiting for my reaction.

"I see," I said again, keeping my voice flat. "Last I heard, the High King was ill, yet still ruling over a time of unprecedented peace and abundance."

"Abundance for who?" Reed snorted. He lay his cards face down and folded his arms on top of the table before looking me in the face. "You care about the people in your service, Margot. That's more than one can say about most of the noblefae in Daybreak. The entire royal family is cruel and corrupt."

"I have to disagree with you, Reed—"

"What is it but corruption to sire ten children, and divide fertile lands that could be used to feed your subjects into massive estates?

What is it but corruption to allow one of the princes to hold an entire court that does not belong to him?" I knew he was speaking of Prince Orist's rule over Serpent Court. I did not respond. I was sure my face had gone completely pale. Reed's voice dropped. "And what is it but cruelty to Bind oneself to a lady and then dump her at an extra house you happen to have, ignoring her attempts to make contact?" Now my face was hot, and my eyes watered. "They have the power to make life better for the fae they rule over, and they choose not to do it," Reed said softly. "What do you call that?"

"I'm tired," I announced, setting my cards down. "I'm going to go to bed now."

"I've upset you," Reed said. "Margot, I didn't mean—"

"It's fine," I lied. "I'm just tired."

"Do you want me to stay?"

"I'd prefer some space, I think." We stood from the table. "I hope you'll come back tomorrow."

"I will," he promised before kissing me. "I did not intend to hurt your feelings."

"I know." But he had. "Goodnight Reed."

The next morning I woke to a large tray of pastries on the table and the fireplace crackling. I was tempted to simply roll over and go back to sleep, but I yawned, stretched my arms, and forced myself out of bed.

There was a notecard folded at the edge of the tray. The shaky lettering said, *I'm sorry* and nothing else. Reed's apology for the previous night, of course. I set the card down and reached for my robe just as a knock sounded on the door. "Come in!" I called as I hastily covered myself. Reed entered swiftly, locking the door behind him. Without a word, he crossed the room and took me in his arms, kissing me deeply.

"I didn't sleep all night," he murmured when we parted. "I hate that I upset you."

"It's alright," I whispered back. "I'm alright. You're allowed to have your opinion—"

"But I should not have implied that you or your family are the problem." He ran his hands up my sides, lingering near my chest.

"Your life has been very different from mine," I said. "I don't blame you for your point of view. It's valid."

"Margot," he choked. "I don't think I can hold back any longer."

"Then don't," I breathed, and I kissed him this time. His wandering hands found the top of my nightgown and groped at my breasts while he kissed me back. A sleeve slid down, exposing my shoulder and Reed's kisses found their way there, then to my neck. We found ourselves backed up to the edge of my bed, where he sat down. I stood between his legs while he pulled my nightgown down with one hand to reveal my breast completely before taking my nipple in his mouth. His other hand wandered under my skirt, caressing my thigh. A moan escaped me as I fell forward into him, wanting to be closer. It was so nice to be desired. To feel wanted.

I straddled his lap, and was moving to remove my nightgown completely, when the door handle rattled. Reed had locked it, thank the gods, so as Arlie began knocking, I was able to quickly straighten myself out while he ran to hide in the bathroom. Hoping I didn't look too breathless, I opened the door swiftly.

"What is it, Arlie?" I asked more sharply than I intended.

"My lady, I am so sorry," Arlie said, nearly trembling, and I instantly felt terrible.

"Don't be," I said. "You just surprised me, is all. What do you need?"

"This came for you, my lady," she said. "I could not find Mr. Cypress, and it looked urgent, so I thought it best if I brought it straight to you." She held out a thick letter containing the Oakshadow seal, and my mouth went dry.

"Thank you, Arlie," I whispered.

"Is there anything I can do for you, my lady?"

"No, that will be all. Thank you." In a daze, I shut my door slowly, leaving Arlie standing there likely very confused. I stared at the letter in my hand, not looking up when Reed joined me again.

"What does it say?" he asked quietly.

My hands shook as I broke the seal and unfolded the thick stationary:

LORD AND LADY OF THE WATERWAYS
Your presence is required at Stag Palace to celebrate the Winter Solstice, in honor of His Majesty High King Edric.
Your host, the Crown Prince Orion, looks forward to your arrival.

Then, in a tidy, looped scrawl, Ever left a handwritten note at the bottom:

Noon, Solstice Eve. Pack something blue.

12

The carriage arrived promptly at midday, as promised. Reed stood a step behind me, ready to place my bags on board and say one last brief farewell before I was to be gone for three days. We had not spent a day apart in all the time I'd lived here and now we were to be separated for what would feel like forever while I played happy wife at Ever's side.

"There's a knife in your boot, correct?" Reed asked.

"Unless it has disappeared since you asked me ten minutes ago, yes," I replied.

"Good. Keep it under your pillow while you're at the palace."

"I'll do it, if only to humor you. I won't need it."

"You never know, Margot. You are his wife, and he has not lain with you since your wedding night," Reed grumbled. "He may decide not to take no for an answer."

"Ever is many things, but he is not a monster, Reed. I'll be fine," I insisted as the carriage door finally opened, and my husband stepped out.

"I just need you to come home in one piece," Reed breathed while Ever approached, smiling warmly. The driver hopped down to assist with the bags, taking one while Reed grabbed the other and walked it to the carriage. Ever bent low, took my hand, and brushed his lips over the back of it for a formal greeting.

"Margot," said Ever kindly. "You look well. That color is stunning."

"Oh, thank you," I said shyly, resisting the urge to examine myself. I wore an emerald green cloak trimmed in white rabbit fur over the top of my dress. Sparrow Court did not have winters as cold as it had been here, so I asked Arlie to send for something appropriate for the wet Serpent Court winters, and this was her selection. "You look quite handsome too." He gave his usual tight-lipped smile, and if I had not known better, I would have sworn a brief flush of red stained his cheeks.

A few more seconds of silence lingered and then Ever said, "Well, we'd better get on the road. Don't want to be late."

"Of course," I said quickly. Ever offered his arm but before I took it, I turned back to Reed, who had placed himself behind me once again. "Thank you, Mr. Cypress. I'll be back soon enough."

"We'll be waiting for you, milady," Reed said with a quick bow of his head. When he looked up again, I saw his face etched with worry. I wanted to kiss him, tell him all would be well— tell him that despite his fear and dislike of the lord, my husband would not harm me. Instead, I nodded once more in Reed's direction before turning to join Ever by the carriage. He helped me up the steps himself before climbing in after me and shutting the door behind him.

We were an hour into our journey before either of us spoke. Ever stared out the window in silence from the moment we were off, and so I matched him, watching the countryside roll by.

"We're a bit more than halfway there," Ever informed me suddenly. "The rest of the journey tends to go quickly from here."

"Good to know," I replied, moving my gaze from the window to my lap.

"Thank you again, for agreeing to all of this," he said. "I hope you've been keeping yourself entertained. How are the hives?"

Irritation rattled me. I had been keeping him well informed on the status of my hives before he instructed me to stop writing to him. "They are well," I said. "We've stopped harvesting for the season, but we'll resume when the frost melts and the bees are more active."

"I'm happy to hear it," Ever replied, and I wanted to kick him. "And what news from Sparrow Court?"

"Nothing more than the usual letters we both receive."

"I do not receive letters from Sparrow Court."

"Why?" I asked bluntly. "You are their lord by right— you should be receiving all the correspondence that I do."

"I do not have authority over the court if I am not present there. My power as their lord lies solely in my marriage to you. You are Lady of Sparrows. That title and authority belongs to you anywhere in the faerie realm."

"Ah," I said, trying to hide my embarrassment. I was so tired of having to have my own court explained to me. Mama never left Sparrow Court, so it had never occurred to me that she was powerless outside of it. "Well then, nothing of great importance. My stepmother is still spending my money as she pleases. I have asked Mr. Dewstone to oversee replanting the flower fields in the spring, to attract the bees, but such things will take time."

"Of course." Ever nodded. "I'm sure all will be well. And if you need your stepmother to be spoken to, I can send someone—"

"That is not necessary, thank you," I said quickly.

"The offer remains." Silence filled the carriage again for a moment and then he said knowingly, "All appears to be well between you and Reed Cypress. I hope your absence won't distress him too deeply."

I blanched.

"Ever— I— I *swear*, we have been as discreet as possible. Arlie and Vic don't know anything. I don't know how you found out, but anything coming from Darkwater is just gossip—"

"Margot— hey, it's fine," Ever said with a slight chuckle. "Your staff are not gossips. Reed's scent is all over you."

"Oh." I was suddenly self-conscious. I lifted my shoulder to my nose and inhaled. I couldn't smell anything but my perfume.

"I didn't consider that your human blood may affect your sense of smell. My apologies for worrying you."

"But— your family. Won't they be able to smell Reed too? Gods, they're going to think I'm some sort of harlot."

"They won't," Ever assured me. "That's just another benefit of the Blood Bond. Traveling in such close quarters, you'll take on plenty of my scent before we arrive. We'll be sharing a suite once again. They'll be none the wiser."

I scoffed. "You've thought everything through, haven't you?"

"You'll come to learn that when it comes to my family, it's best to be a few steps ahead."

"Are they really so awful?" I asked.

"I have little love for Stag Court," he replied.

"That's not an answer."

Ever cocked an eyebrow. "Isn't it?"

"You not loving them doesn't mean they're awful," I said.

"Fair enough," he said. "But yes, most are awful. And there are plenty of them."

"Why attend at all then?"

"I was summoned by the Crown Prince, and no matter how much

I'd like to, I can't ignore that. Besides, it's the High King's favorite holiday, and he likes to have the whole family together. He tries to see the best in them. And there's a handful that I don't mind seeing once or twice a year even if it means putting up with the rest."

"Will I be meeting the High King?" I asked. "I heard he's been ill."

Ever's eyes darkened. "Yes, he's been ill. But the Winter Solstice is very important to him and to the realm. He won't miss it. I'll present you to him when we arrive."

I ran a hand over my hair. "Am I even presentable enough to meet the High King right away? Perhaps I should change first."

"You look fine," my husband scoffed. "It will be better to get it over with now, before the rest of them descend on the palace. We'll pay our respects and retire to our room until dinner." His sharp tone was cutting and made me feel stupid for worrying or even bothering to speak. I knew that tone well, and instantly felt like I was sitting across from my stepmother. My face turned hot, and I turned my gaze to my lap rather than responding. "Shit. Margot, I'm sorry."

I looked up and found Ever studying me. "What?"

"That came out harsher than I meant it. I'm not... I'm not used to sharing the anxiety of all of this. But that's not your fault. I will choose my words and tone more carefully next time. I'm sorry."

"It's alright, Ever. Thank you for apologizing."

"I *am* glad you're here, Margot." He glanced out the window and straightened. "We've arrived."

I looked out the window too and saw the palace rising to greet us as we approached and were covered by the shadows of the gray towers.

There were fae everywhere: arriving in carriages like us as well as walking the grounds. Woodsprites flew overhead, carrying ribbons and sparklers as living décor, while the pathways were lined in candlelit evergreens and white-and-gold pines. The air was festive and reminded me of the solstices of my childhood.

We stopped and Ever moved immediately for the door to climb out ahead of me. He held it open and offered his hand for me to grasp while I stepped down. I noticed a murmur ripple through the fae near me when my feet hit the ground. I took Ever's arm and plastered an adoring look on my face, grinning up at him. He noticed and matched me, starting our performance for those who were already watching us. "Stay close to me," he said softly. I nodded and clung to his elbow as we made our way into the palace.

* * *

We filed inside, following what felt like dozens of fae from the various courts and houses of Daybreak. "The throne room is that way," Ever said, pointing to the left where a handful of people were heading. "We'll go say hello to the king and be on our way before we get sucked into anything with my—"

"Oh, Ever!" a shrill, sing-song voice called from behind us. Ever grimaced as if he knew exactly how obnoxious this interaction would be. We turned to face the most stunning faerie I'd ever seen.

"Hello, Carmen," Ever said flatly, bowing his head. I took that to mean I should curtsy. Carmen's lovely face appeared delighted by our submission.

"Ever," she pouted, "It's been so long."

"Only since Summer Solstice, Carmen," Ever replied. "If I came to every festival in Stag Court, I'd never get anything done."

"Of course," she said. "And we all know how important your work is." Her gaze turned to me. "This must be your Soulbound bride I've heard so much about."

"This is my wife, Margaret Brightwood, Lady of Sparrows. Margot, meet my cousin, Princess Carmen Oakshadow."

"Your Highness," I said softly, dipping my head to greet her. She blinked in my direction before returning her attention to Ever.

"So the rumors are true," she nearly laughed. "You pulled the Lady of Sparrows from her asylum and convinced her to marry you."

"—Asylum?—" I started, but Ever squeezed my hand and I quieted.

"My wife has never stepped foot in an asylum, as you well know, Carmen," Ever replied coolly. "And unlike some people I know," he glanced at a man who stood several steps behind Carmen, who I guessed must be her husband. "She did not take much convincing. I didn't make my match based on what power I would gain or who I could control."

Carmen snorted. "What, do you claim a love match?" Ever just shrugged. He was good at this. Carmen laughed. "You're an idiot." She nearly doubled over. "You're as bad as Soren— though not as bad as Thorn Brightwood, I'll give you that. At least you had the sense not to tie yourself to a full-blooded human." Anger rushed through me and seared into my head so quickly I had to fight the urge to wince at the pain.

"If that's all, Carmen, the High King is expecting us," Ever said flatly. He was clutching my hand again and I could tell he sensed my anger.

"Oh, alright." She waived a dismissive hand. "Go grovel before the invalid—"

"A little *respect*, princess—" Ever hissed, but she ignored him.

"I'll see you both at dinner," she said, and walked away chuckling to herself.

"Wow," I said, staring after her. "She's..."

"A fucking nightmare," Ever finished with a sigh. "Are you alright?"

"I'm fine," I said. "Who's Soren?" Ever stiffened, and while I waited for his reply another wave of pain ran through my head. I winced and rubbed at my forehead in a way that I'm sure looked quite unladylike.

"It's nothing you need to worry about right now. Let's go meet the king."

The throne room only had a few people in it, and none were standing before the throne itself, so Ever and I had a clear pathway to approach. The throne was made of some sort of crystal, or perhaps glass, but the effect made it look to be carved from ice, which suited the Solstice trappings well. More impressive though, was the faerie who sat upon it.

High King Edric appeared stoic and regal with his hands resting on either arm of his seat. The Stag Crown, I suddenly remembered from childhood stories, was not a crown at all, but a pair of antlers growing directly from his head. They would shed upon the king's death, and immediately begin to grow from the head of his rightful heir. I felt myself staring as we approached, and as we did, two things occurred to me: the first, was how much Ever and the High King looked alike. The second was how incredibly old he must be. Fae could live for centuries without any physical aging beyond maturity. Even half-fae like myself could expect near eternal youth. Yet, the High King's hair was dotted with gray, and his eyes had the slightest wrinkles in the corners. Still, he was strikingly handsome. He smiled warmly while we approached. We both dropped to our knees once we reached him.

"Ever... my darling...boy," he said slowly, as if each word were a struggle.

"Warmest greetings, Your Majesty," Ever said. He reached for the king's hand and kissed it.

"Rise... and greet me... properly..."

Ever did as he was told and rose to his feet, pausing to help me up too before stepping closer. He bent low and kissed the High King's forehead. "Happy Solstice, Grandfather."

"Who... have you brought... with you?" he asked, noticing me.

"Grandfather, this is my wife, Margot."

"*Wife!*" The king's eyes sparkled. "I was not... told..."

"It was all very sudden," Ever explained. "I thought I would surprise you in person." Strange, I thought, that Orist would have ordered Ever to marry and be Soulbound, but the High King had no knowledge of it.

Edric gestured for me to come closer, and I obeyed, letting him take my hand when he reached. He studied me for a moment before patting the back of it. "Beautiful...A new... princess...for the realm."

"Not princess, Grandfather, remember?" Ever corrected. "You've made me Lord of the Waterways. And Margot is Lady of Sparrows."

"Not... Thorn?"

"I'm sorry, Your Majesty, no. My father Thorn passed away about ten years ago. I was his sole heir." King Edric blinked at me, then nodded. He kissed my hand again and let go.

"You must forgive... an old man... My memories... are hazy..."

"That's alright, Grandfather." Ever grasped his grandfather's other hand and knelt beside the throne. "Have you had any rest today?"

"I came here... after breakfast..."

"Then you should have some tea and lie down until dinner. How does that sound?"

"I'd prefer... to visit...with Lady Margot..."

"You have wonderful taste in company, Grandfather, but you'll still need your rest for dinner." Ever motioned for a guard.

The High King looked as though he might protest, but I added, "Your Majesty, I do hope you'll excuse me, but I am rather tired after our travels and was hoping to rest myself before dinner." He grinned.

"You both... are working... against me... Fine... rest it is... But I warn you... my lady... I shall expect... much conversation... tonight... I can be... quite... long-winded..."

"Oh, I don't doubt it, Your Majesty," I teased. "That's why I'll need so much time to prepare."

King Edric laughed while his guard stood at attention, waiting for her next order. He looked at her and said, "Alright... soldier... escort me... to my chambers." Ever and the guard helped him to stand, but from there he walked steadily with a golden cane.

I grinned after him, happy that our meeting had gone well. When I turned to tell Ever as much, I immediately noticed red rimming his eyes. "Ever, are you alright?"

He quickly wiped at his face. "I'll be fine."

"Do you want to talk about—"

"No. Let's just go to our room. I'm sure the luggage is there by now."

"Okay," I said, taking his elbow. "Lead the way." Ever placed his hand over mine and squeezed, and I knew that would be as much acknowledgment as I could expect.

The suite we would be staying in was larger than my room at Darkwater, with an enormous plush bed, a sitting area near the fireplace, a reading nook, and a spacious bathroom. I also noted a small balcony through a pair of double doors near the bed. It would be too cold to enjoy the balcony itself, but it would be nice to see the stars through the glass doors while I lay in bed tonight.

"Dinner is in a few hours," Ever reminded me. "It's just family, but, well— you saw out there. There's a lot of them, so just be prepared."

"Are they all like Carmen?" I sat on the foot of the bed.

"Most are not that different from her, but Carmen is her own type of nuisance. It should be smooth sailing from here. She's about as bad as it gets."

"How many are there, exactly?"

"The High King sired eleven children, and each of them have three or four of their own—I'm the only one without siblings— and now my cousins have started having their own children," Ever answered. "So, a lot."

"Isn't it ten?"

"Hmm?"

"You said your grandfather sired eleven children, but isn't it ten? Or did I forget someone?"

"Oh. My apologies. I should have said ten." He busied himself with removing his boots, while I sighed and let my body fall back on the bed as I stared up at the ceiling.

"Why are you a lord?" I asked after a few minutes of silence.

"What?"

I pushed myself up onto my elbows. "Your grandfather is the High King of Daybreak. Your cousin Carmen is a princess— why aren't you a prince?"

"Disappointed with our titles?" he joked darkly.

"No," I said while I rolled my eyes. "I was just curious."

Ever sighed. "The official rule is that only certain members of the royal family can be princes or princesses. If you ask Prince Orion, he'll tell you it preserves the succession, which is already too large." I knit my brow. He noticed, and added, "As it stands today, the law says I'm last in line, and that I am not to be granted such titles."

"That is strange," I noted before lying back again.

"It has been that way for some time now," Ever said. He seemed irritated by my questions, but added, "I'm going to take a bath. Do whatever you want. There are a few books over there if you're interested." He pointed to a bookcase in the corner. "But you shouldn't leave the room by yourself."

Before I could reign in my sarcasm, I replied, "Anything you command, milord."

Ever paused like he might say something in return, but he just shook his head and continued to the bathroom. When the door shut, I let my eyes close with it for a few minutes. I woke in my own bed just this morning when Reed came to say his goodbyes in private. He'd reminded me over and over to be safe. I knew he wished he were here, keeping an eye on me and ensuring my safety around Ever.

Despite our bickering, I knew Ever would not harm me. Our Bond, despite being technically incomplete, would not allow him to even if he wanted, and I had no reason to think he did. But Reed was Reed, and he would want to see with his own eyes that I would not be harmed. I wondered for a moment if I might write him a note. I could send it with a pixie— but the pixie could decide to tear it to shreds or read it aloud to a crowd of ten thousand fae. They were not beholden to the commands of noblefae and requests were barely considered. No, it would be safer just to wait until I went home.

A while later I woke with a sudden jolt. I did not remember falling asleep, and only now that I blinked a few times did I realize my reason for waking: Ever was shaking my shoulder.

"Sorry," he said, when he saw me startle. "I tried to let you sleep for as long as I could, but you only have an hour to get ready now."

I sat up, wiping at my eyes. "I didn't realize I was so tired." I looked around the room. "Did you see where they set my trunk?"

"It's in the other room," he replied. "But I hung your dresses in the wardrobe."

"You didn't have to do that," I grumbled. He shrugged.

"I had nothing better to do. Your cosmetic bag is on the vanity. I didn't open anything, I promise."

"Er, well, thank you then," I said, getting up and approaching the wardrobe. I chose a bottle green gown I'd specifically brought for tonight and spread it out on the bed.

Ever excused himself to the balcony despite the freezing temperature, so that I might dress privately. I quickly touched up my makeup and pinned my hair appropriately before slipping into the dress and realizing my mistake: I'd forgotten about the laces. I couldn't reach to tie them myself, though I spent several minutes attempting it. Finally, I swallowed my pride and held the dress over my body, shuffling to the balcony door. I stuck my head outside and found Ever leaning over the railing with his forearms on the bar. "Don't laugh. I need your help."

He didn't laugh as I thought he might. Reed certainly would have, but then again, he thought most of the clothing worn by nobility to be worthy of mockery. Ever though, had clearly spent time around the complexity of women's clothing. It took him a moment of getting the laces straight, but he had me tied snugly into the gown in no time. "What do you think?" I asked, stepping away from him and turning slowly so he could see the whole thing. I faced him with my hands on my hips when I stopped. "Good enough for dining with the Oakshadow clan?"

"You look great," he said before adjusting his collar in the mirror. I must have had an unsure look on my face because he added, "You look great in everything. And you know I'm telling the truth, so stop fussing and just enjoy making my cousins jealous." I laughed at that. Ever checked the time. "We need to go." As always, he offered his arm, and we were off.

13

Despite his warnings, I did not fully grasp how large Ever's family was until I saw them all in one room. I spotted the eldest of the High King's children, Crown Prince Orion, as soon as we entered the hall. Orion's golden hair fell around his shoulders and a silver circlet adorned with antlers sat atop his head. Like many of the royals, his neck and the sides of his face were covered in large white freckles, resembling the spots on a stag's coat. He was beautiful. They all were.

Orion stood with one of his sisters, talking with a goblet in his hand. He noticed when we entered and raised his drink in Ever's direction, as if to toast him. Ever did not acknowledge it.

There were four long tables in the hall, each large enough to seat twenty fae or so, and by my estimation every seat would be filled.

"Ever!" A deep voice called over the chatter. I followed my husband's line of vision and saw a tall faerie who looked nearly identical to Orion walking toward us. He had a circlet like the Crown Prince's, if less ornate, and a much kinder face.

"Uncle Jory," Ever said happily. He greeted the prince with an outstretched hand, which was ignored and replaced with a crushing hug that forced me to let go of Ever's arm. I stifled a laugh as Ever tried to catch his breath. Prince Jory pulled away but held on to his shoulders as if to get a good look at him.

"How're you holding up with the Serpents? Staying busy?"

"No less than usual, uncle," Ever replied.

"Did Orist arrive with you?" Jory asked, peering toward the door we'd entered through.

"The prince elected to remain at the Serpent Palace again this year," Ever said.

"The lucky bastard," Jory scoffed. "And your house guest?"

"Home for now," he said shortly. Were they talking about Onyx? I got the feeling I shouldn't ask, and while I pondered this, Ever turned his attention to me.

"Uncle Jory, this is my wife, Lady Margaret. Darling, meet my uncle, Prince Jory."

"Your Highness." I curtsied while the prince looked me up and down as if I was his next meal. Somehow, it was charming.

The prince took my hand and kissed it. "The Lady of Sparrows has joined House Oakshadow."

"Indeed I have," I told him with a smile.

He dropped his voice low. "I'll have you know, Princess Carmen is quite stirred up by your arrival."

"Oh," I said. "I, um—"

"Carmen gets stirred up by anything and everything." Ever practically rolled his eyes. "The princess should find better topics to occupy her mind with."

"Can't say I blame her," Jory said. "Whose mind wouldn't be occupied by your lovely bride?" He winked at me. "Lady Margaret, it was an absolute delight to meet you. I must go and make my rounds, but I look forward to getting to know you more soon."

"Likewise, Your Highness," I said. "And friends call me Margot."

"Margot." Jory kissed my hand a final time before shaking Ever's and taking off to greet another group who had just entered behind us.

"Is he one of the ones you like?" I asked.

"Depends on the day," Ever joked. "But yes. Jory is good."

"And the Crown Prince is not?" I murmured.

"Why do you say that?"

"Because I have working eyes," I said. "I saw him greet you, and you ignored him." My voice was low enough that I had to lean in for him to hear me. He made a point to smile slightly when I spoke so that anyone looking would guess we were giggly from being newly Bound rather than discussing which royals Ever despised.

"Orion is not good," Ever confirmed. "Stay clear of him if you can help it."

"I'll do my best," I said. "I don't plan on letting go of your arm until after Solstice, so as long as you manage to avoid him I think I'll be safe —"

"His Majesty, the High King of Daybreak!"

The room fell quiet as King Edric entered slowly, flanked by a guard on either side of him. He paused, and stood near the head of the first table, looking out over his many children and grandchildren.

"My...family..." he began. "It is... as always... my greatest joy... to see... you all together... And it is... my greatest wish...that we become — remain... a beacon of hope...to the...kingdom we serve..." the king continued, and I noticed Ever's attention shift to Jory, who caught his eye. The prince cocked an eyebrow and Ever nodded. Horsing around during the boring part of the evening was a pastime I was well accustomed to, having pulled many silly faces and played nonsense games with other Sparrow Court children while my father addressed a crowd. I turned my attention back to the High King. "...though darkness...surrounds us...the light will... soon return...Thank you."

The room broke out in applause. Ever and a few of his uncles and aunts clapped hard and loud. Jory called out, "Hear, hear!" while Princess Carmen and Crown Prince Orion looked bored, barely tapping their hands together for the sake of politeness.

"Let us sit...eat...and enjoy...one another..." the king added over the noise. He gestured toward the tables and everyone moved toward seats as if they knew exactly where they should go. It seemed there was a routine to all of this. Ever began guiding us to the second table.

"This way," he said, tugging me along while I held his arm. Through the chaos we found our seats— roughly the middle of the second table— but before I could sit in the chair Ever pulled out for me, I felt a hand on my arm. The king's guard from the throne room was standing beside me.

"His Majesty would like a word," she said.

"I'll be over right away—" Ever started but was cut off.

"His Majesty asked for the both of you," the guard clarified.

Ever paused for a second and I could tell he wasn't sure what to make of that, but he quickly regained his composure. "Of course." He gestured for the guard to lead the way while I dug my fingernails into his arm.

"What does he want with me?" I hissed.

"He said earlier he wanted to talk with you tonight. I'm sure that's all it is, I just thought he would wait until after the meal" he said. "Grandfather is harmless. It's his tablemates you need to be careful of."

"What do I say?"

"You can say whatever you want, just know they'll be ready to pick you apart no matter what."

"You're so comforting," I grumbled as we arrived at the table, greeted by the smiling king. I curtsied.

"Oh good…" King Edric started. He stood, despite my attempted protest, and kissed my hand. "I hoped…you both…would join me…I want…to get…acquainted…with my…newest granddaughter." I blushed furiously and bowed my head both out of gratitude and in an effort to hide my face, which I was sure would be as red as my hair.

"I would be honored, Your Majesty, thank you." Ever echoed my thanks and we sat in a pair of empty seats to the right of the High King, which put me right between Ever and his grandfather, and directly across from Princess Carmen and Crown Prince Orion. Looking at them closely now, I noticed how similar the pair's features were to one another and I realized they must be father and daughter. With as unpleasant as my first encounter with Carmen had been, I was not looking forward to interacting with Orion.

I chatted with the king more easily than I'd expected I would. He spoke so slowly, and occasionally mixed up names and titles, but he was funny and curious, and seemed quite interested in what I had to say. It was after the plates from our second course were taken away and replaced with the third that Orion finally spoke. His deep, gravelly voice made me think he would be more at home in a court of wolves than a court of stags.

"Tell us, my lady, why is it you've hidden away so long?"

"Hidden away, Your Highness?"

"This is the first we've all seen of you, yet you've held your title for over a decade. Since becoming Lady of Sparrows, there have been plenty of opportunities for you to come to court and pledge your loyalty to the crown. Yet it was not until you married my nephew that anyone this far from Sparrow Court laid eyes upon you. Why?" I blinked at him. The question was blunt, and demanded an answer, but he was not aggressive. He took a bite of his food and chewed while looking at me expectantly.

I opened my mouth to speak, but Ever cut me off by telling me, "You do not have to answer him."

"Of course she does," Carmen snapped. "The *Crown Prince of Daybreak* asked his subject a direct question—"

"Court governors are subjects of the High King, and are required to answer only to him, not his offspring who forget their manners and interrogate a dinner guest," Ever snapped back.

Orion chuckled and leaned back in his seat, flashing a wolfish grin.

"My apologies, lady, if like your husband you deem my question an interrogation. It was not intended as such." Gods, the men in this family were charming.

"Oh— of course not, Your Highness." Then, to answer his original question I said, "My stepmother, Lady Wilda, thought it best if she handled court on my behalf," I half-lied. "I had a difficult time after my father's passing, and I was so young..." I trailed off, letting their minds fill in what I did not say. "Only a few months ago I took on the full scope of my duties."

"I see," Orion said before taking another bite and chewing slowly. He swallowed, and added, "I must admit I find myself disappointed with your explanation."

"Your Highness?"

"I would have hoped that, perhaps, even at such a young age, you would have been wise enough to know that someone with your tainted lineage couldn't possibly expect to effectively govern a court of Daybreak." He said it with such a calm, matter-of-fact tone that it took me a few seconds to understand what he'd meant.

"...*Tainted*, Your Highness?" I asked. I felt the blood leave my face. Carmen was smirking at the pair of us while I felt Ever silently fuming beside me. Orion remained casual.

"It's no secret that Thorn Brightwood shocked and disgusted the realm by taking a human as his bride." The Crown Prince laughed in earnest now. "And then to breed with it and make the offspring his *heir*—"

"*Enough.*" Ever's tone was harsh enough that it made me flinch in my seat.

"I'd merely hoped that the girl had enough sense to let Lady Wilda handle things, and that was why she'd snubbed the palace, but I was wrong." Orion shrugged, and turned his attention back to me. "Of course, it's not your *fault*, my lady, but the fact remains that your parentage is undesirable at best. Still, you've managed to charm the High King and your husband, and undoubtedly with the cut of that dress—" His eyes flicked to my chest and in an instant, I felt so dirty that a year-long bath would do me no good. "— my brother Jory. So, clearly, your intellect is not entirely lacking. I'll be interested to see how clever you turn out to be."

I wanted to say something back. Something cutting and witty that would at least make me feel good if it didn't hurt him. Instead, I sat there in stunned silence while Orion turned his attention to Carmen

86

and her husband as if nothing had happened. Hot tears pricked in my eyes and threatened to spill over when Ever quickly leaned in and murmured, "Don't give him the satisfaction." He tucked a curl behind my ear as casually as he could. "We cannot leave while Grandfather is still eating. As soon as he stands, I'll get you out of here." I nodded once, with as little movement as I could manage, and turned my attention back to my plate, though I didn't eat another bite.

Ever kept his promise, and as soon as the High King bid us all a good night, he whisked me back to our suite without saying another word to anyone. When the door shut behind us, I let out a long, shuddering breath and let the tears well in my eyes once again. I had to catch myself on the back of an armchair to keep from stumbling. Ever stood at my elbow, hovering as if he might need to catch me. When I calmed, he spoke quietly, "Margot, I'm so sorry."

"I've never heard someone talk like that before."

"It's completely inexcusable," Ever said.

"Does everyone in Stag Court think those things? About my father — about humans?"

"No. Not everyone."

"But it's a common opinion?" I asked, finally turning to face him. His expression was grim. "Ever."

"Most fae are indifferent to humans unless they want them for sex or labor," he admitted. "But some are hostile to humans and those with human blood."

"Why wouldn't my father have told me this?"

"I imagine he wanted to protect you."

"No one in Sparrow Court has ever said anything," I said mostly to myself. "Not even Wilda, not my stepsisters…"

"Humans had been living peacefully in the west for long before your father took his place as Lord of Sparrows," Ever said. "Sparrow Court has always been a gentle place to live. Laws about human welfare were in place well before your mother fell through the faerie ring that brought her to Daybreak." I couldn't tell if Ever was being thorough in his explanation or if he was rambling to keep me from crying. "Your father was kind. Most subjects of Sparrow Court are— well, save for Wilda and her daughters." He chuckled, and I managed a little smile. "The royal family has a lot of backward thinking members. I'm sorry you were exposed to them tonight. I will do everything I can to keep it from happening again."

I nodded and crossed my arms over my chest, taking in his words. I had just one more question on the topic. "And the High King? Does he hold the same views as his son?"

"No," Ever replied firmly. "He's very old, and I doubt he was always very progressive when it came to human matters, but I have never heard him utter a bad word about humans or half-fae. I swear."

"I suppose there's nothing to be done but bear it then."

"I'm sorry," he said again. "I wish you didn't have to hear things like that."

"Thank you," I said. "It's not your fault though."

"I know. I'm still sorry."

We let silence linger between us for a minute before I asked, "So what's on the agenda for tomorrow?"

"Nothing official before the ball," he answered. "Was there anything special you wanted to do?"

"It would be nice to get out of the room for a bit, but to be honest I don't know how many more royals I can handle meeting." Ever snorted, which surprised me.

"You and I both," he said. "Don't worry, I'll ensure that you are entertained for the day."

"Why does that sound like a threat?"

"Who said it wasn't?" he teased.

I rolled my eyes and left him standing there while I made my way to the bathroom. My night bag was sitting near the sink, and I managed to reach back and loosen my dress enough to shimmy out of it and change into a nightdress and robe. I was suddenly struck with the feeling that I'd experienced this before— the night of my wedding, preparing to share a bed with Ever. This time of course I knew what to expect, knew Ever better, and that I would not be bothered in the night by him. Still, there was a strange feeling in my belly. Excitement, maybe? The feeling we were getting away with something. Guilt, that I wasn't with Reed tonight? Gods, it had only been this morning that I saw him but so much had happened that it felt like it had been days.

Ever was on his side of the bed, legs stretched out in front of him with a book in his lap. He'd placed a long pillow on the center of the large mattress as a dividing wall.

"I kept your lantern on," he said without looking up. "Wasn't sure if you wanted to stay up and read or just go straight to bed."

"I'm going to sleep," I said through a yawn. "It's been a long day."

"Do you want me to read by the fireplace?" he asked, reaching for his lantern as if to extinguish it.

"No, I don't mind a little light," I told him. He nodded and left it alone while I put out my light, shrugged off my robe, and climbed into bed.

I lay on my back with my eyes closed, trying to find sleep when that same, strange sensation occurred in my belly again. This time I did recognize it to be guilt, but not about Reed. I'd been so angry at Ever for ignoring me, for leaving me alone at Darkwater, that I did not stop to think how hard this marriage must be on him. Every moment with me, in front of his family, having to behave as if we're Soulbound— it meant he could never publicly have anyone else. I knew I couldn't either, but somehow, knowing he'd chosen that for himself to help a stranger seemed like such a bigger sacrifice than me accepting as my last resort. Did Ever love anyone? Could he, knowing they'd never get to be the one on his arm at the palace?

"Ever?" I said, opening my eyes to stare at the ceiling.

"Hmm?"

"I'm sorry that you have to be married to me."

"What?" he asked. I heard him close his book but couldn't bring myself to look over at him.

"I just— I can see that this is not an easy thing, and I'm sorry that you've had to put up with so much on my behalf."

Ever seemed to consider his words before replying, "I didn't have to be married to you, Margot."

"I know, but—"

"You know that I was ordered to marry and Bind myself to someone."

"Yes," I said.

"Well, I'm glad it was you. It is... much easier to do this with someone that I admire," he said.

Then perhaps you could reply to my letters, I wanted to snap. But instead, I told him, "I just don't want you to miss out on happiness with someone because you're attached to me."

"I won't," Ever said. "I'm not looking for love, Margot. It's not exactly my thing."

Now I turned my head toward him with what I was sure was a confused look on my face. "Not your *thing*?" He shrugged. "Do you just not *feel* love, or—"

"I do," he said, sounding like he was regretting telling me anything. "I have. I'm just not looking for that right now."

"What about comfort? Companionship?"

"There are many ways to get...*comfort*," Ever said. "And I have an overbearing aunt and a bratty wife for companionship, what more could I need?" He didn't wait for a response before putting out his light and lying down on the other side of the pillow wall. The bed shifted as he rolled, turning his back to me.

"I didn't mean to offend you," I said through the darkness. "I only meant that... if it's something you want one day, I hope you get to have it."

Ever sighed. "Thank you. No offense taken. Love is just not something I can see for myself... But I'm happy for you, that you've found it with Reed."

I didn't have the energy to explain that I wasn't in love with Reed, so I let his words hang in the air. I didn't know what it was I had with Reed. A distraction from my duties, yes. A companion to stave off my loneliness, absolutely. More than friendship...but not love. Not yet. I didn't want to think about it too much.

"We should get some sleep," Ever said. "Another long day tomorrow."

"Are you going to tell me what you're entertaining me with?"

"Not a chance." I heard his grin in the darkness. I shook my head as I shut my eyes again.

"Goodnight, heartless husband."

"Goodnight, bratty wife," he chuckled. And with no more harsh words between us, we both settled into the darkness and soon fell asleep.

14

"Ever, I *really* don't like this."

"Come on, it will be fun."

Ever woke me a little after dawn, instructing me to put on the clothes he laid out at the end of our bed. He was sitting in an armchair, lacing up his boots, buzzing with all the excitement of a child. I didn't bother with a robe and marched to the bathroom with the clothes bundled in my arms. I nearly laughed when I unfolded the items. They were Ever's clothes. Long, thick gray pants hugged my wide hips tightly but bunched around my ankles as I was at least six inches too short for them. Next was a plain white shirt and a deep blue knitted sweater to go over it. I had to roll the sleeves up once I had both on so I could use my hands. I tied my hair into a quick braid before joining Ever again.

"I look like I'm shrinking," I told him with my hands on my hips.

"You look perfect. Put those on." He pointed to a pair of snow boots that looked about my size. They were sitting in front of one of the armchairs while a pair of thick socks lay on the table between us.

"Whose boots are these?" I asked as I sat and reached for the socks. "Where are we going?"

"It's a surprise."

"What, the owner of the boots, or...?"

"Hush."

I grumbled under my breath about the early hour and the cold weather while I pulled the boots on and laced them up. Ever practically tapped his foot while he waited impatiently. "All set," I told him once I was done. "Now what?"

"Now, we hurry so we don't miss out on a good spot." I joined him by the door where he held open a brown coat from who knew where. I slipped my arms into it and shrugged it on before we rushed out the door.

Now, I was sitting on the front of a wooden sled, with Ever behind me. His hands were on the ground, holding us steady as the nose of the sled peeked over the edge of the steep hill we were at the top of.

"If you let go of me, I'll fucking kill you," I said as I gripped the edges of the wood, tight enough to turn my knuckles white beneath my mittens.

One of his hands left the ground and snaked across my middle. "You're going to love this—"

"*No!* He beat us!" A voice yelled from behind us. We both turned and saw Jory, accompanied by a few royals I hadn't met yet coming over the top of the hill.

"Ever always gets the first drop!" one of the women complained. I could see the tips of her ears poking through her golden hair, already red from the cold.

"That's because Ever gets his ass out of bed!" Ever called over his shoulder. "Better luck next time!" The arm over my middle tightened and he pushed off, sending us speeding down the hill so fast I couldn't muster an audible scream. The wind and snow whipped me in the face, stinging against my skin as we raced down, down, and eventually wound up on flat ground, where we sped forward until the sled slowed and we came to a stop.

Ever let go of me and stood to climb off the sled. I followed suit and when I faced him I was met with the biggest grin I'd ever seen plastered on his face. "What do you think?" he asked. His uncle and cousins began speeding down the hill on their own sleds. Ever picked ours up off the ground and we began trudging back to the top.

"I think you're all insane," I said. Ever laughed. "But this is quite thrilling."

"We do it every year at the Winter Solstice," he explained. "It started with my father and Jory. Then my aunts Olenore and Melina found them out and demanded they be allowed to join or else they'd tell Grandfather." He pointed at a pair of princesses sharing a sled nearly flying past us. "There they are," he said. "Grandfather knew already of course, but my father and uncle let them join in anyway. It was just the four of them forever, until a handful of cousins started joining and soon it turned into this." He gestured to the lines now forming at the top of the hill, with perhaps fifteen members of Ever's family taking turns on their sleds.

"I'm guessing these are all the ones you like?" I teased.

"Of course they are." Ever laughed. "You think you could get Carmen dressed like that and out here in the cold?" I laughed at that too.

A few seconds later we were in line, and when it was our turn Ever did not hesitate again. He held things steady while I took my seat, then he pushed while his feet were still on the ground, getting a running start before jumping on the back and grabbing hold of my torso as we flew down the slope. This time when we reached the bottom, I was grinning right along with him. I paused for just a moment to shake the snow out of my hair before racing to make it to the top again while Ever trailed behind me with the sled.

We carried on for hours. Teams formed at some point in the mid-morning and races became the game of the day. Ever and I won several times in a row. Then I won again at the front of Jory's sled but lost on the back of a cousin's whose name I never learned.

It was after lunchtime, and most of Ever's family members were filing back to the palace while we were setting up at the top of the hill again.

The whole morning I'd seen a different, carefree side of Ever that I never had before— that I doubted most had before. I watched him fool around with his cousins, dropping handfuls of snow on their heads and making them shriek. He'd gotten into a playful argument with Jory that ended in them tackling each other into the snow. He'd been joking and laughing with me all day, letting his competitive nature and craving for adrenaline rub off on me. The truth was, Ever was fun to be with. I'd had more fun earning a chapped face and frozen hair with him than I'd had in years.

"Last one, then we'll call it a day," Ever said from behind me.

"Fine," I half-whined, though the thought of going back to the warmth of indoors was rather enticing. "Make it a good one."

"Hold on tight—" Ever pushed off with his feet again and jumped on, but he gripped the edge of the sled instead of wrapping his arms around me. We were going too fast. Somehow, we'd ended up on a slick of ice instead of the powder we'd been sliding down all day. Ever was barely crouched behind me, completely unstable in his position. He could tell what happened too, and tried to sit properly to help regain control, but the movement caused the sled to tip, and he flew off the side, landing in the snow. "To the right!" I heard him yell. I listened, leaning to the right and the sled followed suit.

Too fast. I was still speeding downhill too fast. Then suddenly, a huge snowbank was rushing toward me. I braced for impact and let my body slam into a wall of packed snow and ice. My face smacked against it, and I blinked away the involuntary tears that came when my nose felt the hit. For a moment I just lay there, staring up at the gray sky.

"Margot?" Ever called. His footsteps approached. "Margot!" He spotted me and rushed over to kneel beside me. "Are you alright?"

"Yes," I groaned as I sat up. As soon as I did, blood rushed from my nose, and I began to laugh.

"Fuck," Ever breathed. He reached under his clothes to his innermost shirt and ripped a strip off to press against my face. "Margot, honey, I'm so sorry—" His shoulders shook, and I realized he was laughing too. We both sat there, laughing hysterically while he tended to my injuries until I couldn't sit up any longer and fell against him, still unable to catch my breath. His hand rested on my back and I felt him run his palm up and down a couple of times like he was trying to warm me.

When we got ahold of ourselves, I sat up and said, "Thank you for this, Ever. I've had fun today."

"Me too." He reached forward and knocked some snow off my shoulder. He stood, then offered his hand. "Let's go get you warmed up. I'll send for food and we'll get ready for the ball."

I took his hand and stood. "Oh, yes. That."

"It truly isn't terrible. We'll drink ourselves silly, watch Jory flirt with anyone who has a pulse—maybe even dance once or twice."

"I can't wait."

Ever bathed while we waited for our lunch to arrive, and after we ate I started the tub for myself. Ever said he would dress and then pay a visit to Jory's suite for a drink while I got ready, so I would have the room to myself.

I poured drops of plum oil into the steaming tub before stepping in, only allowing myself to relax with my head against the edge for a moment before I began scrubbing my skin and hair. The hot water eased my aches from this morning and got my blood pumping, ready to attend my first Stag Court ball— a rite of passage I should have taken a decade ago when I came of age.

A couple of hours later the sun was going down which signaled that the party was beginning. I only needed to hook earrings into my lobes to complete my work. A knock sounded, and when I bid him to enter, Ever strode through the door with a drink in each hand, stopping short when he'd fully entered the room.

"Wow."

"What?" I asked, fastening the second earring and looking down at my skirts. "Is it too much?"

"Not at all," he said, swallowing. "You look beautiful." I felt my face immediately turn bright red, and Ever handed me one of the drinks.

Though my nerves plagued me, I managed to mumble a bashful "Thank you" then added, "You look really handsome too, Ever." His midnight blue jacket was luxurious, embroidered with filigree in the same shade so you only saw the stunning artistry if you were really looking. Paired with black pants and formal black boots, Ever looked every bit the handsome lord. I would be on his arm in a shimmering gown of ice blue that flattered my hair and, apparently, made my husband stop in his tracks.

Ever raised his glass. "To us," he said. "On our first Solstice together, managing to pull this off without killing one another." I laughed, and he added sincerely, "And to you, wife, for agreeing to all of it in the first place. Happy Solstice, Margot." I softened. We touched the rims of our glasses together and drained the contents.

"Happy Solstice, Ever."

15

I entered the ballroom on Ever's arm, and the sight nearly took my breath away.

Nearly a hundred fae had descended on the palace for the Solstice ball, all dressed in beautiful, sparkling clothes. A smirked to myself, noting that no one in the glittering crowd had the tall hairstyles or colored ear powder that my stepmother and her daughters had insisted were in fashion here in the capital.

The same evergreens and white pines that we saw outside yesterday were in each corner of the ballroom, so tall they reached the ceiling. Each one was decorated to capacity with candles, ribbons, dried fruits, and bells. More evergreen boughs were placed strategically around the room, while bundles of mistletoe hung from the ceiling, waiting for lovers and acquaintances alike to be caught beneath them. Pixies and woodsprites darted above us, seeming to have a party of their own as they danced and spun, flinging fairydust from their wings as they did. The best part was the floor-to-ceiling windows that lined the far wall, showing the beautiful winter scene outside as gentle snowfall continued, illuminated by the bright full moon.

"Wonderful, isn't it?" Ever said in my ear as I gawked at the room.

"It'll do," I joked, but my voice gave away my excitement. "Ever, this is amazing."

"If the palace does one thing right it's throwing a good party." He looked around the room. "Let's say hello to Grandfather."

We approached the High King's dais, which was also decorated with pine and candles. The slight, contented smile on the king's face as he watched the festivities unfolding grew into a wide grin when he saw Ever and me.

"Ah... my...stunning...granddaughter...returns..." Tonight, I leaned forward to kiss his cheek after I curtsied.

"Happy Solstice, Your Majesty."

"Grandfather," he corrected with a wink. Then he spotted Ever. "My... darling boy..."

"Happy Solstice, Grandfather," Ever told him with a bow and a kiss to the other cheek. "Though, how happy can it be, when it seems my wife has outshined and replaced me in your eyes?"

The king lit up at the joke and his deep laugh rumbled like a much younger faerie's. He squeezed Ever's hand. "My affection...for you... could never be...replaced...only...added upon...by your lovely... bride..."

"I know, Grandfather."

"Now...both of you...stop humoring...this old faerie...and enjoy... the festivities." Grandfather grasped my hand and pressed my knuckles to his lips. "Your High King...commands it..."

We each bid him farewell, and as we stepped off the dais to join the party, I caught the eye of Orion, who was staring at Ever and me with deep disdain.

"I need a drink," Ever announced, ignoring his uncle and guiding me toward a servant with a tray. He handed me a goblet before taking one himself and drinking deeply. "It's no Sparrow Court mead, but it does the trick."

I took a sip and was delighted by the flavor of spiced plums. I was tempted to drain my goblet in one gulp but decided to savor the festive wine instead. I was about to comment on how much I liked it when Jory came bounding toward us, dressed in a suit of deep cranberry. Before I could greet the prince, he was kissing my hand.

"My Lady of Sparrows, you are a vision of winter starlight."

"Happy Solstice, Your Highness," I replied, blushing. Ever rolled his eyes.

"Uncle, you are shameless," he said.

"I've never denied that." Jory winked at me. "What's there to be ashamed of?"

"Flirting with a married faerie seems like a good start to the list."

"She's married to my nephew—"

"That's so much *worse*."

"Keep his glass full tonight," Jory told me. "Between you and some good wine, it seems Ever may manage to lighten up after all."

"I'm sure you'll manage to keep things light enough for all of us," I replied. Jory grinned.

"Gods, I like her," he told Ever. Then, a pause, as if he'd only just remembered something. "Er, I must tell you, nephew, that some feathered friends were asking if they might speak with you tonight."

Ever turned his gaze somewhere behind me in the ballroom. The music and dancing was just starting to get rowdy, so it appeared that Ever was simply watching the party unfold around us.

"It's a bit crowded for that, don't you think?"

"They have traveled far," Jory said. "It must be important." Ever hardened his jaw.

"They should have waited for a night less festive." He sighed. "Tell them to pay their respects to the High King and his heir and be on their way."

I watched them back and forth, waiting for something either of them said to make sense. It never did, though it all seemed rather important. I wondered who their friends were, but by the look on Ever's face I thought it best to wait until later to ask. Eventually, Jory bid us farewell, making me promise to dance with him before the night was over. Now that it would not appear so obvious, I turned to watch Jory leave. He paused to greet people here and there before making his way to a pair of winged fae standing along the other wall. They were dressed in black suits that I imagined would keep one warm while flying but stood out against the sea of bright dresses and glittering suits. They were both dark haired, with enormous black feathered wings coming from their backs which they kept tucked in, trying, it seemed, to stay out of everyone's way.

"Friends of yours?" I asked.

"Visitors from Nightfall," Ever said. "I have some business with them but I don't understand why they would come here."

"That is strange," I said. "It's Solstice. You'd think they would wait for another day."

"You would think," he repeated. "Would you like another drink?" I shrugged, and after promising he'd be right back, Ever took my empty goblet and walked away in search of a servant to replace the wine.

I stood alone for a moment, watching the party, when I was approached by Princess Carmen and a pair of fae women who looked quite like her that I did not know.

"Ah, it's the Lady of Sparrows," said Carmen sweetly. I blanched. "And the Waterways, I suppose, if you count that."

"Who would?" one of the women laughed. I curtsied to Carmen and ignored the insult.

"Happy Solstice, Your Highness."

"Indeed," she said. Then, motioning to the women beside her she added, "These are my father's sisters, Princess Lura and Princess Naexi." I curtsied again, greeting them both despite their sneers.

"She's exactly as you said," the fairer one, Lura, said to Carmen. "So human. Fascinating."

"If it weren't for the ears, I'd never guess she had even a drop of fae blood," Naexi added.

"I have quite a few, actually," I said, despite their insistence that they speak about me as if I weren't in front of them.

"Of course you do," Carmen said. "And what an example you are to the rest of us, Lady Margaret."

"Sorry, what am I an example of?" I asked, glancing around to see if Ever approached. I couldn't find him anywhere in the crowd.

"Maybe *warning* would be a better word than example," Lura suggested.

"Quite right, princess," Carmen agreed. "A warning of what happens when you dirty noblefae blood with that of a human." Unlike the night before, I was expecting some comment or another from Carmen, so it did not catch me off guard as her father's comments had. Still, I felt my face get hot and the three princesses began laughing amongst themselves. Where was Ever? I couldn't leave them without reason, and I desperately needed one.

Prince Jory appeared almost out of nowhere and now stood offering his arm to me. I took it, and Jory addressed the princesses. "Sisters. Niece. Good to see that your opinions and manners remain as horrifically outdated as your appearance."

"Uncle." Carmen's smile was barely more than her bared teeth, sharp and glinting in the candlelight. "Good to see that you remain a drunken mess, of use to no one."

"Indeed." He looked down his nose at them before turning his attention to me. "This drunken mess needs a dance partner. Would you be so kind, my lady?"

"Of course."

"Come along then." Jory led me on his arm away from the princesses without saying goodbye— something I would be punished for if it weren't for him. When I thanked him for saving me, the prince waved me off. "Those three are forever searching for someone to be cunts to. You're just their target for Solstice. It's the least I could do."

"Why do Carmen and Orion hate me so much?" I asked.

Jory sighed. "It has nothing to do with *you*, my dear. Some of my siblings and their children have awful opinions about humans. They believe they should be second class citizens. Half-fae, in their eyes, are the product of disorder. Especially when the half-fae is among the nobility. I don't believe Daybreak has ever had a half-fae governing lord— or lady. They see you as a threat, and an insult, to the way things ought to be."

"And you?"

"What about me, lady?" Jory's eyes sparkled at the question.

"Do you find yourself hostile to humans?"

"Would I be preparing to dance with you if I did?"

"That's not an answer, my prince." The corner of Jory's mouth quirked upward.

"I think humans are wonderful," he said. And with that, he spun me onto the dance floor, and I couldn't help but grin. A full ballroom on Solstice. It had been ages since I felt this. A few minutes of joyful revelry with Jory was exactly what I needed to rid myself of the cloud that hung overhead following my encounter with Carmen. It wasn't until Jory nearly shouted over the music, "Your husband approaches!" that I remembered I was waiting for Ever.

"Having fun?" he asked in my ear. I spun to face him.

"I'm certainly managing it without you," I replied. "Luckily Prince Jory was here to keep me entertained." Jory bowed and kissed my hand theatrically. "Do you dance, husband?" Ever bristled.

"Of course I dance," he said stiffly.

"Then ask your wife to dance." I laughed, and Ever softened.

"Will you dance with me, Margot?"

I nodded and took his hand. Ever spun me a few times, and once he allowed himself to smile, to relax and enjoy himself, we both sank into the celebration. Just us, and the hundred other souls surrounding us, welcoming the return of the light.

16

It was nearly midnight when Ever and I found ourselves stepping away from the dance floor, trying to catch our breath.

"Why is it so hard to stop dancing once I've started?" I asked, not really expecting an answer. Of course, Ever had one:

"Most likely it's your human blood. Humans cannot stop dancing to fae music on their own. Not unless they're removed from the dance floor by a faerie."

"Charming," I said, and I remembered all the times I saw my parents dancing together, how Papa always seemed to guide Mama around. I never thought much of it before now.

"It's cruel, old magic that should have been done away with a long time ago," Ever said. "Sorry, I shouldn't have mentioned it."

"You don't need to apologize," I told him.

"Someone ought to."

"Perhaps I should just get used to the answer to all my questions being, *your human blood*," I joked, and Ever huffed a laugh.

A low whistle sounded, and our attention turned to Jory, who was sauntering past us with a pretty faerie on his arm. He disappeared a few minutes after Ever joined me on the dance floor and just now showed his face again. "The newlyweds owe the gods a kiss!" he called out with his hand cupped around his mouth. We must have looked confused because Jory pointed eagerly above our heads: hanging over us as we stood before one of the giant ballroom windows, was a bundle of mistletoe. Ever looked back at his uncle and shook his head.

"No."

"Oh, go on!" Jory yelled, and now more fae were turning toward us, laughing and clapping excitedly when they saw what dangled above our heads.

"They aren't going to stop, are they?" I asked, nearly laughing at how ridiculous they were all being.

"Probably not," Ever said. "Sorry. We can just go—"

"I'd like to stay," I protested. I glanced up at the mistletoe again. "They just want a quick kiss and they'll shut up, right?"

The fae were chanting *"Kiss! Kiss! Kiss! Kiss!"* Even the drunken woodsprites and pixies joined in the applause, flying around in crooked formations.

"Yes— but, Margot, it really isn't necessary."

"I don't mind if you don't." I shrugged. "What's the harm?" Then, after a few seconds of staring down at me, Ever shrugged too. *"Kiss! Kiss! Kiss!"*

"Sure, what's the harm?" he repeated, and smiled.

Ever placed his hand on my arm and bent down to meet me. The chanting grew louder and more excited. When we met for the expected, brief brush of our lips, the chanting stopped and those watching erupted into cheers— and then silence. I could no longer hear them, could no longer focus on them or anything other than this kiss that had not stopped. The effect was immediate: heat, static, longing, and fear of what would happen if we parted. I wondered for only a second if it was just me—if I was dragging it out for too long and embarrassing myself. As soon as the thought entered my mind it was gone, because Ever's hand left its friendly perch on my shoulder to cup my face, sliding back just slightly for his fingers to grip into my hair. His other hand found my waist and pulled me tightly to him, and I wished there was some way to get closer. There was a sharp pricking, like a needle in my heart, tightening a stitch. My hand rested on his chest just as Ever deepened the kiss, forcing my lips to part when his tongue brushed over them. He tasted sweet, like plum wine. He tasted like stars. Like home, and the only thing tethering me to reality.

Eventually, we had to breathe, and I cursed the gods for giving me lungs that required air— as if anything could sustain me as well as this. We both gasped for breath, not moving from where we held one another. Ever's hand remained on my face, and I felt his thumb brush my cheek as he stared down at me, eyes wide and pupils blown.

"What..." I started. Words would not come to me.

"I don't know," he replied, chest heaving. "Are you alright?"

I nodded. "I think so—" I was cut off by a terrified, blood-curdling scream.

It came from the center of the ballroom. None of the fae that had been chanting for Ever to kiss me just a moment ago were near us. They had all flocked toward the commotion.

"What is it?" I asked.

"I don't know," Ever replied. He took my hand in his own. "Stay close." We pushed through the crowd until we found Jory, standing at the edge of the dance floor. He was seething with rage and looked very pale. I followed his gaze and saw what he was staring at: a box— no, a cage—in the center of the room, covered with a black silk cloth as if someone were preparing to set a table. Princess Carmen was dragging her fingertips along the cage's edge while she spoke, addressing the gathered fae.

"... now the old king's gone to bed, and the *real* festivities can begin!" She laughed, and so did most of the fae around her. Her wild joy filled me with dread. "Friends, my father the Crown Prince and I wracked our brains for ideas, trying to think of suitable Solstice entertainment when my garden was treated to this little pet!" Carmen ripped back the cloth, laughing when the crowd broke into excited cheering and inside, a naked human girl screamed again.

She did not appear to be very old, though I was not always sure of human ages. She was not a child. I could not imagine she was much older than twenty years, but her tearful face and cowering form made her look younger. I was going to be sick.

"Let's go," Ever said in my ear.

"No," I said. "We have to help her!"

"We can't." He discreetly gestured to the room. The gathered fae were becoming hostile. Violent. Some were laughing, some bared their sharp teeth as they waited excitedly for the princess to continue. "There's nothing we can do."

Carmen snapped her fingers and the cage disappeared, resulting in another scream, followed by more laughter. "Come out, come out, little pet," Carmen crooned, stooping in her dress to put her face an inch from the girl's. The girl hid behind her hair. She crossed her arms over her breasts and squeezed her eyes shut. I couldn't look away. Carmen tilted the girl's chin upward, making her long, black hair fall away from her face. "Open your eyes, little worm." The girl's lip quivered, but she did as she was told. "There, there. All will be as it should."

"Please– I want to go home. What is this place? Please."

Carmen grinned. "No, little worm. You won't be going home."

"We need to go. Now." Ever was still gripping my hand. The other was on Jory's arm. The prince had his hand on his belt, reaching for a dagger.

"*Help her.*"

"I cannot interfere."

The girl cried as Carmen dragged a fingernail down her cheek, splitting it open. Blood poured from the wound and mixed with her streaming tears.

Suddenly, another faerie was beside us. It was one of Ever's aunts, Princess Olenore, who I had met that morning. "We need to get him out of here." She motioned to Jory who had not taken his eyes off the scene before him.

"I'm trying."

Carmen's voice pierced the air and my attention returned to her. "How do you feel, little worm?" To my horror, more cuts lined the girl's face. She was barely recognizable; her skin was soaked completely red, and she was on her knees. When the girl remained silent Carmen's fist gripped her hair. "I asked you a question."

The girl sobbed, "*I want my mother—*"

Carmen twirled, utterly giddy with her game. She paused only once, to curtsy in the direction of the throne, where I saw now for the first time that Orion was seated there, ankle over knee, with a goblet in his hand and a bemused look on his face. "Oh!" Carmen stopped, putting a theatrically worried hand to her cheek. "I'm being rude, aren't I? Hogging all the fun." She waved and a door flew open. An ill-looking servant carried a lead attached to a collar around the neck of another human. He was blindfolded, and from the back of his collar there was a chain attached to the collar of a very old human woman, and the same chain attached her to another girl about the same age as Carmen's first victim. They were all shaking in fear, naked, with their heads turning about at the sounds of cheers and snarling faeries. "Worms for all!" Carmen shouted, presenting her gifts to her audience. "Enjoy yourselves, and Happy Solstice!" She descended upon the first girl, and just as she was about to bring the point of a dagger to her skin, I felt a rough hand grip my chin and turn my face away.

"Don't look!" Ever ordered sharply. "Just look at me, Margot. Keep looking at me until I tell you to go. Olenore is going to get you to our room. Lock the door and don't open it for anyone, do you understand me?" I nodded. "I have to get Jory out of here," he explained, and I noted Ever's tight grip on his uncle's arm. Jory was straining against him. "I will come to the room when he's secure. *I will not knock.* Do not open the door for a knock."

I nodded again. Ever looked beside me and dipped his chin, and then there was a new hand on my elbow. "Come on," Princess Olenore said in my ear. "They've all gone absolutely fucking mad." She whisked me through the crowd of bloodthirsty fae, avoiding contact with them as much as we could. The screams from the crowd and their human victims combined practically shook the enormous windows. Olenore and I made it to a door, and despite myself, I turned back to look for just a second and saw two things I would never forget: the first was the human girl, now lying flat on top of a new table, completely flayed. Her wide, lidless eyes stared blankly up at the ceiling while she gasped for breath, unable to move aside from the involuntary shivers and erratic rise and fall of her chest while her body fought desperately to keep her alive. Curious, vicious faeries stuck their fingers in between her exposed muscles, separating the strands and ripping the tissues as if they were strips of paper while they continued to peel her apart bit by bit, then sticking their fingers in their mouths to taste her blood.

The second, was when I glanced toward the throne, perhaps in hope that I would see the High King appear upon it and put a stop to all of this, but instead found the Crown Prince leaned back in his seat while he continued sipping his wine and chaos unfolded around him. For a second, I thought he looked right at me and smiled, but Olenore was dragging me away before I could know for sure.

It turned out we were not the only ones escaping the horrors of the ballroom. The corridors were filled with dozens of faeries running toward their suites, putting as much distance between themselves and Carmen's antics as they could. Olenore kept her arm around my shoulders, guiding me quickly through the dim palace. Still dazed, I only noticed where we were when someone stopped Olenore right outside my door.

"Ollie, what the hell—"

"I don't know, Mels—It's completely out of control."

"Where is Jory?" The faerie—Mels— asked sharply.

"Ever has him. They're both alright. Just get to your room and lay low until morning."

"I will, I'm just checking that the children made it back. Should I check in on yours too?"

"Please," said Olenore. "Tell them I'm helping Ever and we'll talk tomorrow."

"Of course." The other faerie left as quickly as she'd come. Once she turned a corner, Olenore checked up and down the hallway before opening my door and ushering me inside.

I stood, unable to move, in the center of the suite while Olenore checked behind doors and curtains, looked under the bed, and ensured the windows were locked. When she finished, she opened the wardrobe and found my nightdress. She set it down on the bed before coming back to me, and I did not stop her when she stood behind me and began to loosen the laces of my gown. She helped me to step out of it before bringing the nightdress down over my head. Still, I felt frozen, replaying the images from the night in my mind. I couldn't even muster up a thank you. Olenore bid me to stay where I was while she went to the bathroom. She returned with a bowl of warm water and a cloth and began wiping the makeup off my face. "That feels better, doesn't it?"

I nodded.

"Would you like me to braid your hair?" she asked. I nodded again, and she brought me to my bed to sit. The princess climbed up behind me and pulled the red mass of curls out of my face before she started separating and weaving it.

I picked at my nails with shaking hands in the silence until I finally got the nerve to speak. "What's wrong with Jory?" I asked quietly.

"The same thing that's wrong with you, lady. All of us. Watching that horrid mess—"

"Of course," I said. "But Jory seemed very effected. More than the others."

Olenore sighed. "My brother has always had a soft spot for humans. We were never sure what it was. Curiosity, I suppose. It was his curiosity that led him to Meghan. His wife."

Wife? I thought of Jory's flirtations, of the pretty faeries he danced with tonight. Not that the princes of Daybreak were known for their fidelity, but— "She died," Olenore continued. "About fifteen years ago. Old age," she added before I could ask. "The dear lived until her ninety-eighth year, which I'm told is quite a length for humans. By all measure, they were blessed with what they got: eighty years together. Four children. A happy life, no matter how brief."

I was stunned. Jory had a human wife, and half-fae children.

Suddenly, "But, how could he bring her somewhere like *this*? How could he raise children around people who would hate them so severely?"

"He didn't," Olenore clarified. "Carmen's display tonight is a new level of wickedness, even for her. But attitudes about humans were not much better when Jory and Meghan met. They wed and remained at his country home on the edge of Sparrow Court until she died. Only a few of us even knew about Meghan and the children. Jory let the rest of Stag Court believe he'd gone on a century-long bender. Ruined his reputation to keep her safe from court. He doted on her, adored her absolutely until the last minute," she said. "The girl tonight looked just like Meghan did when she first arrived in Daybreak." Gods. I was shaking again and fell back to silence. I wanted to vomit. "There," Olenore said before I could get too worked up. She tied the end of the long braid with a ribbon. "All done. Let's get you to bed."

"I should wait up for Ever," I said.

"You've had an ordeal, Margot. He'll want you to rest. I'll stay and watch over you until he returns." I had no energy to argue with the princess, so I gave up and did as I was told. She helped me climb in under the covers, then put out the lamps until the only light in the room was the fireplace and the bright, cold moonlight pouring in through the balcony window.

As I began to drift off, I couldn't help but think that, no, I had not had an ordeal. I stood and watched— we all had— while horror unfolded before me. The shame and grief in my gut turned to silent tears as I wept until my eyes could not hold themselves open any longer.

I woke briefly to the sound of hushed voices, but I could barely open my eyes. Squinting, I made out Ever's form removing his coat. Muffled whispers reached me as I dozed: "How is she?"

"I believe she may be in shock."

I drifted in and out until I felt Ever get into bed beside me, rousing me enough that the weight of the night fell on me once more, and I began crying all over again. I tried to stay quiet, but my shoulders shook, and my tears were joined with small, gasping breaths that gave me away. Ever's warm, gentle palm fell lightly on my arm and I flinched, pausing for half a moment before letting the loud sobs finally escape me. Ever did not say anything or try to quiet me at all. Instead, he wrapped his arm around me, pulling my body to his chest to hold me while I cried myself back to sleep.

I woke up again while it was still dark. There were still a few hours until sunrise. Ever's deep breathing filled the room and only after I was awake for a couple of minutes did I notice his hand was still on my arm. I shrugged out of his touch and quietly rose from the bed. Olenore was nowhere to be seen, and, not wanting to sit alone in the dark, I decided to put my robe on and step out onto the balcony to watch the snow fall.

I settled onto a bench seat, sitting sideways so I could pull my legs up and watch until the clouds parted and the stars came out. I didn't look up when the door opened, or when Ever placed a blanket in my lap before sitting across from me. I didn't look to see if he was watching me or the sky, but eventually I spoke first.

"Mama told me the stars are different here." Ever shifted in his seat but did not speak. "The moon looks the same, but the phases are different, too. She told me that she didn't really believe she was somewhere else until she noticed the stars. They're all mixed up. The constellations are different. That was how she knew she was truly in another world." Ever's face was filled with pity. I hated him looking at me like that. "She must have been so scared."

"Lady Grace was blessed to have found Lord Thorn," Ever replied. I scoffed.

"I don't think it was a blessing. More like dumb luck."

"I met them both, Margot. They loved each other and had a good life together. And they loved you."

"I know they did," I said. I turned my attention back to the stars. I wasn't sure what point I was trying to make. My head was swimming.

"Would you go there, if you could?" Ever asked, looking curiously at the sky. "To the human realm?"

I shook my head. "The only place I did belong... Well, I was cherished there until I wasn't. And then it was only my people remembering me that kept me going. Knowing that one day I would reclaim the power of my court and the sparrows would know me as their lady kept me tethered to my home. And now—" I swallowed, and my voice fell to nearly a whisper. "Now I have proven myself a coward, unworthy of that power awaiting me, and I— I fear even the sparrows have forgotten me."

"That's not—"

"I sat there while those humans were torn apart," I said bluntly. "I am not worthy of my position. The sparrows will know, and they will forget me now." I wiped at my eyes. "No, I don't belong among the humans any more than I belong among the fae. I don't belong in my court anymore. I don't think people like me were meant to belong anywhere."

"Margot."

"The most powerful fae in Daybreak called my blood dirty to my face. I took it, and the next day they tortured those humans for party entertainment." Ever didn't reply. "My father was good to his people, human and fae alike. He was so good— too good— at protecting me. I didn't know until my stepmother cursed me that anyone would think to use my human blood against me. I had no idea until tonight that any of it was this bad. My father left me completely unprepared for the reality of my position."

"Margot—"

"I think I'll go back to bed," I interrupted, setting the blanket aside as I stood.

"We'll leave before midday," Ever replied. "I wanted to go earlier, at dawn, but I won't allow any more palace staff in here. We'll have to pack our own bags. I've arranged for one of my carriages to come for us."

"Fine."

"You'll be back with Reed before dinner tomorrow."

Gods. Reed. I hadn't had a single thought of him today. From the moment I woke I was engrossed in the palace, in befriending Ever. I'd been distracted by sledding— had that only been this morning? By dancing. By that kiss. Reed warned me to keep myself protected here. He was right. He was right about this whole wretched place. He'd been right about nearly everything.

I didn't respond to Ever. I just walked back to bed and climbed in. I rolled on my side to face the far wall so I would not have to face him. He remained outside for another few minutes before I heard him enter and latch the balcony door. I felt him get in bed and roll away from me as well, so our backs faced one another.

"Ever?" I said into the darkness after some time had passed. He was so quiet I wasn't sure if he was still awake.

"Hmm?"

"I'm never coming back here with you." A long silence followed, leaving my words hanging in the air.

"Okay."

17

The next morning was silent except for the sounds of us packing our trunks. We met our carriage and driver at the same gate where we'd arrived. The decorations were still up, but none of it seemed particularly festive anymore.

I moved to grab my trunk handle but Ever reached it before I could. He and the driver lifted it onto the back of the carriage, and once it was secure it was time to go.

"My Lady of Sparrows, I hope you don't plan to leave without farewell." I turned. Jory approached, looking exhausted, but he held a smile for me anyway. When he reached us, he took my hand in both of his own. "I'm sorry my nephew is rushing you to travel so early, but it is for the best."

"It's me who's rushing, uncle." His eyes lit up when I called him that. "I have a lot of work to do at Darkwater. My staff will be missing me."

"You are living at Darkwater now?" He asked Ever.

"No," said Ever. "I'm not." Awkward silence followed while Jory looked between us.

"Ah. I see. Well, I wish you both a safe journey," he said. "And Margot, darling, feel free to write." He winked and kissed my hand before letting it go.

"Please give His Majesty our regards and apologies," Ever said. "I will come to see him again soon."

"Of course." Jory bowed strangely— a bit too deeply to be casual, but I knew the prince was probably clumsy from exhaustion. He waved as we took off, and I waved back through the window before settling into the silent journey home.

When we arrived, Reed came out of the front door quickly, nearly running to meet us. He seemed relieved when I stepped down from the carriage, accepting Ever's offered hand. Reed looked me over, probably checking for injury.

To no one in particular, he said, "We weren't expecting you until this evening."

"We thought it best to return early," Ever replied. "It was an exhausting couple of days." He moved to help the driver with my trunk.

"Are you hurt?" Reed murmured when Ever was out of earshot. "You're pale as a ghost."

I shook my head. "Nobody hurt me," I said. "I'm just glad to be home."

"That should be everything," Ever announced when my belongings were off the carriage. "My driver will take it inside for you—"

"We can manage, my lord, thank you," I said.

I half expected him to argue, but instead he glanced over at Reed before replying stiffly, "Well then, this is where I leave you." He bowed his head slightly. "You know where to find me, if you need anything."

"Thank you, my lord."

Ever climbed back into the carriage, hitting the roof twice as he did, signaling to the driver that he should go. I watched until they disappeared, and Reed asked from behind me, "Margot, what the hell happened to you?"

My breath went ragged, and I fell to my knees, landing in the dirt as I wept. Reed gathered me in his arms, lifting me up to carry me inside while I wailed into his chest. He carried me all the way to my bed and tucked me in before lying down and letting me curl into his side until I fell asleep and remained there the rest of the day.

18

I didn't come downstairs until dinner the following day. Arlie greeted me carefully when she set my plate down before me. I planned to eat quietly and return to my bedroom, but after a few bites I found tears slipping down my cheeks. Every twang of my fork against the plate sounded like the human girl's scream. Like the fae chanting for Ever and me to kiss. Like my own mind calling me *coward, coward, coward—*

After only a few minutes I pushed my plate forward and left the table, my forgotten napkin falling from my lap to the floor as I rushed back upstairs, trampling the linen.

Reed came to my room a few minutes after I'd let the door click shut behind me. I was curled on the bed. Shallow, gasping breaths escaped me, and I struggled to get myself under control. He sat beside me and soon I was lying in his lap, squeezing my eyes tightly shut only to see flashes of the girl's flayed body behind my lids, and Prince Orion smiling at me from the throne. I didn't even know that girl's name. No one in the ballroom did. Every witness to her death, every faerie who caused it, had no idea what she was called. She had a home, in the human realm. A family. Parents, maybe siblings, friends, who would never see her, never know what happened to her— but perhaps that was a blessing.

"You're shaking," Reed murmured, running his hand up and down my arm. He shushed me gently.

"I'm sorry," I said. "I'm sorry that I went at all."

"Do you want to talk about it? Did he— your husband—"

"Ever didn't do anything to me," I said. "Like I told you, no one hurt me." I didn't want to talk about Ever. Especially not with Reed. Our budding friendship had been squashed by the events of the

Solstice ball, and now I hardly imagined I would see my lord husband again, if either of us could help it. That thought made me sadder than I wanted to admit.

"I'm here, if you need someone to talk to," Reed said quietly.

"I think I just want to take a sleep tonic," I told him. He nodded. "I'll tell you everything in the morning." Reed moved me from his lap and stood.

"I'll go fetch the tonic," he said gently. "Change into your bedclothes and I'll be back in a few moments."

He left and I did as he said. I left my dress where it fell, even though it had barely been worn for an hour and pulled a nightdress over my head before lying back on the bed, trying desperately to rid myself of the memories that plagued me, and the shame that accompanied them.

Reed returned with a pale blue bottle in hand.

"Here," he said. "Vic keeps this in the cupboard with all the medicinal herbs. He said it'll make you sleep like the dead, and I gathered that's what you want."

I nodded, accepting the bottle gratefully. "Thank you," I said and then took a long swig.

"Careful," Reed said and took the bottle back. "Too much can be dangerous."

"Thank you," I said again. "For looking after me."

"Someone needs to, don't they?" The corner of Reed's mouth tugged upward, then he bent down to kiss me. He pressed his lips against mine, and while I didn't mind it, I could not bring my mouth the be anything but a cold, hard line. If he noticed, he did not show it. "Get some rest, Margot." Reed tucked me in and left my bedroom as oblivion overtook me.

The next day was better, if only slightly.

Arlie came in early to drop off a tea tray and refresh my water pitcher. I peeked beyond my eyelids and watched her add a log to my fireplace before picking up the dress I'd left on the floor the previous night. She seemed unfazed, but guilt roiled in my gut. What a selfish thing, I thought. It would have been nothing to pick the damned dress up and put it in the wardrobe, and now Arlie was adding my laundry to her list of tasks for the day. As if she didn't have enough to worry about. I thought of stopping her but knew my arguing would only embarrass her and I did not want that either.

When she left, I dragged myself upright and dug the heels of my hands into my eyes, rubbing the last bits of sleep out. I poured tea and donned a pale green robe before sitting in front of the fireplace, staring at the crackling flames. I could have found a book, or started doing something useful, like looking over any letters from Sparrow Court I'd missed over the last few days, but I just kept my gaze on the fireplace, enthralled by the flames licking the sides of the new log and the destruction of the old ones.

I'd been sitting there for almost half an hour when Reed came to join me. He held a small plate with a pastry on top. He set it down on the table beside me and said, "From Vic. It's cinnamon and dayberry." I looked down at the pastry but did not reach for it. "You need to eat something, Margot."

"I will," I said, though I wasn't sure if it was a lie. I took a sip of my lukewarm tea and hoped that would satisfy him for the time being. "I suppose you want to hear the story now."

"I would like to know what happened to you, yes," he said.

I sighed, and without further hesitation, told Reed about my arrival at the Stag Palace, meeting the High King, dinner on Solstice Eve with Ever's family, and all that happened the night after, at the Solstice Ball. I did not bother telling him about sledding with Ever, Jory, and the others, nor did I tell him about dancing and drinking spiced plum wine with my husband. Or finding myself under the mistletoe with him. It was all an act anyway, keeping up the façade of our marriage, but I would keep those small pockets of joy tucked away in my memories.

I knew his thoughts about the nobility weren't generally kind, but mere mentions of certain names caused disgust to paint Reed's features. He did not seem shocked by my description of what happened to the human girl. He almost seemed to scoff, as if her fate were something obnoxious done by the noblefae rather than the horror it was. When I finished, doing my best not to shake, I drained the dregs of my teacup and set it on the table beside the dayberry pastry I still hadn't touched. My finger ran along the edge of the plate, tracing hand painted roses.

"I'm sorry you were witness to such things, Margot," Reed finally said. "The royal family are monsters."

"Some of them," I agreed. "Perhaps most of them. But some are good, too." I told him about the kindness the High King and Prince Jory showed me, and how Princess Olenore looked after me.

"And yet the system they represent allowed for the Crown Prince and his daughter to sanction human slaughter for party entertainment."

"I know what you think of the royals and the courts," I said. "I was just saying that some of them were kind to me. The Oakshadows are not born evil, Reed."

"Fine," he replied with a sigh. "My apologies. It's just hard to hear you recount their monstrosity and not say anything. I cannot believe your husband didn't step in."

"He said he couldn't interfere," I explained. "He did not tell me why."

"Because he's a coward. All noblefae are."

I turned to face Reed. "Ever is not a coward. You do not know him well enough to even suggest that. Though it is good to know where I stand in your mind." I did not add that I agreed with him, about my own cowardice.

"Obviously I wasn't talking about—"

"If you do not think me a coward, then you think I am a monster," I said. "I cannot help the nature of my position any more than you can. In fact, my title is probably the only thing that let me leave the palace unscathed."

"I didn't mean to anger you," Reed said softly.

"I know you didn't. I just… it's been a long couple of days. I should probably get back to bed," I said.

"Do you want me to stay for a bit?" he asked.

"No," I said, reaching for my tonic. "Arlie will notice if you stay too long."

Reed looked disappointed. "I'll come check on you tonight."

I nodded. "Thank you," I told him. "I'll try to be back to my old self tomorrow."

Reed stood and kissed my head before moving to leave. "I look forward to it."

Each day that followed was easier than the one before it. I learned to keep my memories at bay during the daytime, and within my first week back at Darkwater I was able to bury myself enough in all the work I'd missed that I did not have time to dwell. Reed began to visit me again after dinner.

The first time, it was just to wish me goodnight and brush a swift kiss across my mouth, but by the third night he was staying to play cards with me. On the fifth, the kisses lasted longer, and we wound up lying on top of the covers of my bed, hands tangled in each other's hair. When he moved to palm my breast, I stilled and moved his hand away.

"Are you alright?" he asked.

"Yes, I'm fine, I just— I don't want that tonight."

"Oh," he said, sitting upright. "I didn't realize."

"I know we were moving in a certain direction before I left," I said, propping myself up on my elbows. "And I plan to continue that, I just... need some more time to readjust. I'm sorry."

He shrugged. "I can be patient," Reed said. "The reward will be worth the wait."

I smiled and lay back again. "If you still want to stay, I would be glad to have you here." He let out a long yawn.

"Perhaps it is best I go to my own bed." Reed planted another kiss on my mouth. "Another night," he promised before slipping out the door.

He tried again the next three nights, each time I turned him down. Reed's face was patient, but I could tell by his strained voice that each time aggravated him further. One night, after a particularly brutal hand of cards in which he won twenty copper pieces, Reed kissed me in celebration, lingering just enough for me to know what he wanted. He nuzzled his face into my neck, nibbling at my jaw. "I'm sorry, Reed," I said. "I'm exhausted."

He looked crestfallen, and said quietly, "I've missed you, Margot."

"I know. I've missed you too. I just need some time to—"

"You were gone two days, I don't see how that requires this much readjustment," Reed snapped.

I gaped at him. "I—I told you what happened there. What I saw—"

"You witnessed something horrid. Most people I know would want comfort after an ordeal like that."

"If you want to comfort me, you may. I just don't feel like having sex with you right this minute."

"Sex with *me*? Interesting choice of words, Margot."

"Oh be quiet," I said with a roll of my eyes. "You're being ridiculous."

"Am I?" He was on his feet. "You just spent two days with your *husband*. His scent was all over you. It still lingers now, weeks later."

"We are Bound, and we shared a suite—"

"Of course."

"Reed, get out." I pointed to the door and shock washed over his features. "I'm not talking about this anymore."

"Fine." He stormed toward the door. With his hand on the knob he added, "Forgive me for wanting to know why you came home to me acting like a different person."

"Then perhaps you should have paid better attention to my explanation. Instead, you threw a fit and made accusations because I wouldn't fuck you the second you asked."

"That's—"

"Goodnight, Reed."

"Milady." The word was paired with a sneer on Reed's face, followed by the slam of my bedroom door.

Without changing out of my clothes, I lay on my bed, staring at the ceiling until I fell asleep. It crossed my mind that I should be upset, or even angry. I didn't feel much of anything.

19

I thought Reed and I would settle our fight by breakfast, but when I went downstairs I was met with near silence, except for Arlie, who greeted me as usual. Reed stood in his proper place, holding the letters I'd missed while I was away. I hoped that after he read them to me he would stay, that he would apologize, but he simply excused himself and left to get to work.

It went on like that for a week. Reed said nothing to me unless he was required to by reading me my morning letters. I held firm, assuming he would give in eventually and come to me asking for forgiveness for his outburst. Instead, in the middle of the second week of this, Reed stopped reading my letters to me at breakfast. He left the sealed envelopes on the silver mail tray, and Arlie explained on his behalf that he had too much on his list of daily tasks to continue doing this for me.

Before I knew it, more than a month had passed and Reed had hardly said a word to me. No word had come from Ever either, and with Reed's silence I quickly found myself lonelier than I'd been when I first arrived at Darkwater.

Enough time had gone by now that I found myself desperately missing Reed's company. Our fight had been so stupid— I'd let my emotions about the Stag Palace, about my time with Ever, get in the way of what I could have with Reed. Perhaps it could have been something more than fun, more than distraction, and I'd ruined it with my complaints, with my hesitation. But now, so much time had passed that I did not know how to fix it, or if I could fix it at all.

The days continued, and I was delighted when the weather warmed enough for me to go and visit the hives in the afternoons. The bees were slowly emerging, but with few flowers blooming yet, they remained close to their home, preparing for the work to come in the spring. When the ground began to melt, I was able to open the cellar door and go down to check on the mead. The cellar had done its job and remained warm through the winter, which meant the jars of mead had continued fermenting as they should have. All was well and I should have been happy. I couldn't help but wish, however, that Reed was checking this progress with me, excited for what the new year would bring. As I stood in the warm cellar, looking around at all my hard work— in the place where Reed first kissed me, no less— I decided enough was enough. I had to talk with him. I had to apologize for how I'd treated him.

When I emerged from the cellar and let the door fall shut, I spotted eyes looking at me from the tree line. The woodsprites were awake, but not ready to brave the open air, opting to stay within the slightly warmer protection of the trees. I waved a hand in greeting, but none of them moved. "Sorry," I called, though I knew they couldn't understand me. "No honey yet. A few more weeks." As if they understood every word, the woodsprites' eyes began disappearing as they all darted back into the forest. When I finished talking with Reed, I would head toward the kitchen to look for a jar to send along to them.

Once I was inside, I washed myself and changed into a clean lavender dress, a simple piece, but warmer than many I owned. I found Reed in his office, going through stacks of papers and looking irritated. I stood in the doorway and knocked on the wall. "Hello," I said quietly when he looked up.

"What can I do for you, milady?"

"Nothing," I said. "Just… wondering what you're up to."

"I'm going over our inventory. The sentries and salt harvesters return next week but we still have a month or so before the garden produces anything worthwhile."

"Oh," I replied. "Will we be all right? Should we send for supplies in town?"

"We'll make do." He held up the stack of papers. "There's a lot to be done here, milady, if there's nothing else—"

"Reed." He stared, waiting. "Reed, I'm sorry."

"Are you?"

"I am. I'm sorry I was so cold to you when I came home from the palace. It was all just... more than I expected. I shouldn't have pushed you away like that."

"No, you shouldn't have." Reed sighed. He set his work aside and rubbed his hand over his face. "I told you I would be worried while you were gone and then you come back and you just... you shut me out and sent me away."

"I know I did," I said. "Reed, I'm so sorry. Can you... can you forgive me?"

"Margot... I don't know how you expect me to answer that."

"Reed, please—" I felt my throat tighten and my eyes go hot. "I just want to make things right. Nothing has been alright since I left for the palace. Please. Just— let us have dinner together. We'll walk the shoreline after, and play cards, and— and everything can be how it was."

Reed stood from his desk and crossed the room. When he reached me, he brushed a tear from my cheek. "Don't cry."

"I can't help it," I said shakily. "I miss you."

"I know," he said softly, and he pulled me into his chest. I nearly sobbed with relief and buried my face in his shirt. "I know. It's alright, Margot," he murmured into my hair while he smoothed his hand over it. We parted and he kissed me.

"I'm sorry, Reed," I said again.

"Let's forget all of it," he suggested. He glanced back at his desk. "I still have quite a bit of work to do. I'll see you at dinner?"

"Yes," I said. "But not as my steward. Join me at my table."

"But— Arlie..."

"Arlie will be discreet," I assured him. "It looks like I'll be living here a long time. I refuse to hide you from the others any longer."

Reed smiled at that. "Alright then. I'll see you at dinner."

20

Arlie had indeed gone a bit wide-eyed when, after pulling my chair out for me to be seated at dinner, Reed took the spot to my left. But, as I predicted, she said nothing and simply brought two plates. Reed grinned through the whole meal, and I couldn't help but do the same. We hardly spoke, but it felt so good to be back to normal.

After, we were preparing to walk the shoreline as I'd suggested earlier, when the wind blew through an open window and chilled me, even though I'd just put on my coat.

"My gods!" I exclaimed, pulling the collar up around my neck. "It's freezing!"

"Spring takes a while to arrive here," Reed chuckled. "Even as the days begin to warm up the nights tend to freeze over. You can thank the lake for that."

"I'm not going out there without my gloves," I said, and reached for my coat pocket. It was empty. "Strange." I patted the other one. Nothing. "I usually just keep them in the pocket, so they don't get lost."

"I'll run upstairs and see if I can find any," Reed offered. "I wouldn't mind getting some for myself now that I think of it." He kissed my cheek and bounded up the stairs. I glanced toward his office, where the door stood open, and I noticed one of my scarves tied around the otherwise empty coat rack.

"I'm going to check your office!" I called after him, but I did not know if he heard me. I stepped inside, took my scarf, and tied it on before looking over Reed's shelves and cabinets to see if I'd set them down some time ago. When I did not find them, I checked the top of his desk. Nothing. The top drawer. Nothing.

I opened the bottom drawer, and still my gloves were nowhere to be seen. Just endless letters that had been opened and folded up again before being tossed carelessly into the drawer. I shook my head, with plans to tease Reed about his lack of organization, when something caught my eye. The broken seals on the letters were all dark green with a pair of antlers pressed in the wax. The Oakshadow seal.

Puzzled, I grabbed a letter at random. On the front of it a tidy scrawl read:

Lady Margaret Brightwood
Darkwater House
Serpent Court

My hands shook as I unfolded the page:
My Lady,
It seems you grow busier by the day. I hope you'll find time to respond soon — I want to know how you are settling in.
I am at your service.
Best Regards,
Ever

I opened another one:
Lady Margot,
Thank you for your diligent updates on the state of Darkwater. It is a relief to know the estate is in good hands. I am delighted to hear the hives have settled in well for you. Your samples were appreciated and enjoyed.
I am at your service.
Warm Regards,
Ever

Another, this time from the very top. When I checked the date, I saw that it was received just three days ago:

Margot,
I don't even know if you're reading these. I'm sorry. For everything. I'd like to know if you're alright.
The Equinox is coming soon. Will you visit?
As always, I am at your service.
Ever

122

"I couldn't find your usual pair, but I found these. Should be fine for a walk around the— what are you doing?" Reed was in the doorway with a pair of my gloves in his hands. I stood behind his desk, with Ever's letter, and apparently every letter he'd written to me since my arrival at Darkwater in the drawer below. There must have been fifty of them. "Why are you in here?"

"I saw my scarf," I said softly, shaking. "I thought my gloves might be here, so I opened the drawer... Reed, what is this?"

"Margot, I can explain—"

"Then start explaining. Why do you have my letters? *Why did you let me think Ever wasn't writing to me?*"

"I know what this looks like, but you have to understand—"

"You... you hid them. But he said—" The wheels turned in my head as realization crashed down upon me. "You wrote that letter, didn't you? You pretended it was him telling me not to write."

Reed was quiet. If he were capable, I would think he was taking his time to come up with a good lie. Instead, he let out a breath and shook his head at me.

"Damn you, Margot. I was so close."

21

"Go fuck yourself, Reed," I spat, and threw the letter down on the desk. I stormed toward the door, intending to stomp past him, but he put his arm up to block my way. "Let me out and go pack your fucking bags. I want you out of my house in an hour."

His arm moved, but instead of clearing the doorway for me to leave, Reed's hand met my chest and shoved me backward, hard enough that I slammed into the desk. Stunned, I stared up at him as he shut the door.

"Do you know what it's like," he began calmly, "To care for the home and possessions of spoiled, rich noblefae who have nothing better to do than count their money and look down on you for no other reason than a lack of status?"

"I've never—"

"My family already had too many mouths to feed before I was born," Reed continued over me. "My parents only had half the number of children your precious High King did, and still, not one of us had a full belly a day in our lives. Meanwhile, the line of succession grows stronger every year as your husband's family fucks and spits out more heirs to inherit more land, leaving fewer and fewer resources for the rest of us."

"Reed—"

"I thought I struck gold when I was hired here," he chuckled. "I'd never been a steward of course. I forged my papers, got fake letters of recommendation. It's not like the nobility can be bothered to check that sort of thing. The closest I'd come to managing a household was running the kitchen at a shithole inn up north." I was awash in disbelief. His entire demeanor had changed. All of Reed's decorum was gone as he seethed. "It was going to be easy. Manage the house for some lord's wife, collect the pay, maybe pocket an extra coin here and there if I found it. Then, Lord Oakshadow dropped you off here and I saw you, looking like a doe-eyed imbecile, trailing along after him while you practically begged for any crumb of his attention, and a thought crossed my mind: if the Lord of the Waterways would pay for an entirely separate house and staff simply to look after his wife, what would he pay to retain his own honor?"

"What did you do?" I whispered.

"You let me do everything for you." Reed shrugged. "It was easy enough to hide the letters, re-write them so it looked like your husband was rejecting you... whatever I needed to do to make you believe that the faerie who Soulbound himself to you was utterly indifferent to your existence." He choked on a cruel laugh. "Gods— I know you're only half-fae, Margot, but truly, it was shocking to see how easily you believed this shit. I put his letters away once I'd opened them to make sure he wasn't planning a visit, and I sat back and watched as you handed over your stupid little reports, week after week, waiting for his praise. I was going to let you keep looking for it until you gave up, but honestly it was painful to watch someone be so incredibly pathetic.

"I showed you kindness. I gave you attention. I pretended to be interested in your boring stories and aroused by your pudgy human body. I made you moan like a whore—"

"I don't understand. I did nothing to deserve this," I said. I felt my mouth quiver like a child and hated myself for it.

"That's the point," Reed snapped. "You've done nothing to deserve *this*—" he gestured to the rest of the house. "—except be sired by a rich lord and fucked by an even richer one."

"You wanted to be cruel. To embarrass me," I said, wiping away the hot tears on my face. "Well, you've achieved your goal. Congratulations. Now get the hell out of my house."

"No, Margot, my goal has not been achieved." I blinked at him, and he sighed. "I suppose this is what I get for playing the long game. My goal was to take you to bed and put my bastard in your belly."

"I—I don't—"

"*I don't understand!*" he wailed in a mocking, high-pitched tone before rolling his eyes. "You told me your husband only demanded discretion from you. Another faerie's baby carried by his wife is far from discreet. The gold your husband would have had to pay for my silence would mean I'd never have to work again."

"So what will you do?" I wiped angrily at my face again. "With your plan ruined, how do you suppose you'll make your fortune now?"

Reed let out a long sigh. "I thought it was fairly simple, if a bit messy." I looked at him blankly. "You really are so fucking dense, Margot. Why do you think I bothered explaining myself? So you could write up a little report for your husband?" He laughed harshly. "First, I'm going to kill you. That should be obvious. As far as my fortune goes, it's not as if anyone will be coming to check up on you. I have plenty of time to strip every room in this gods-forsaken house of its valuables before anyone notices anything is amiss." His voice and words were chilling, and I was suddenly very aware of the fact that he stood between me and the doorway. "I'll admit you were sweet. Not bad to look at, either. I'll grant you a quick death if you don't fight me."

My eyes darted to the doorknob, and, stupidly, I ran straight to it, hoping that if I took Reed by surprise, I might be able to open the door and scream for help. Instead, the back of Reed's hand met my face so hard that it nearly knocked me off my feet. I doubled over in pain, and he grabbed my hair, holding it at the scalp as he yanked me back up and turned me to face the other direction. He took the ends of my scarf in his hands and pulled, cutting off my airway. My hands clawed uselessly at his, trying to loosen his grip. When my vision began to go fuzzy, my muddled thoughts gifted me one last idea, and I slammed my heel down as hard as I could on top of his foot. Miraculously, I startled him enough to make him let go. I turned to face him, and just as he was about to reach for me, I shot my knee between Reed's legs, driving it up as hard as I could. It was his turn to double over as he cried out and caught himself, smacking the top of the desk. Without a second thought I picked up a silver letter opener and plunged it right into his hand, pinning him to the desk before I threw open the door and bolted out of the office. Reed's angry scream echoed behind me, and I knew that he would not be giving up his pursuit.

I looked at the front doors. My first instinct was to sprint, but even with a head start Reed would catch me if he were to give chase. I could go through the kitchens, through the back door, but then I might put Arlie or Vic directly in his path. There were no sentries on the grounds. No one who could help me. I heard Reed struggling in the office, maybe working up the nerve to free himself of the letter opener. I looked around frantically, trying to decide what to do. The stairs. I could lead him upstairs, trap him in my study, then make a break for the stables. Once I was on horseback Reed would have no chance of catching me. At full speed I could be at Ever's house in less than an hour, and I would be safe.

There was no time to think of anything else, so I moved for the stairs, stomping my feet as I went, making sure Reed would follow me and not go searching elsewhere, putting Arlie and Vic at risk.

I was at the top of the landing when Reed stumbled out of the office, his hand bleeding freely at his side. He was coming straight for the stairs, soaked in rage. I ran down the hallway, slamming random doors as I went so he might stop and look for me in the wrong rooms.

I made it to my bedroom, shut my door, and locked it. I shoved a chair under the doorknob after attempting to block the entrance with the wardrobe but found it too heavy. I ran to my study and locked the connecting door behind me.

Reed was breaking doors in the hallway. Good. I managed to buy myself a few seconds. I started to look around for a weapon— a knife, another letter opener, anything I could jab him with quickly before locking him inside and running again. Nothing, nothing— my desk was clear. I threw open the drawers and dumped them out on the desk's surface. Only a few pens and loose paper. Then, hidden among the blank pages so I nearly missed it: a small white drawstring bag. I remembered Ever's words the day he dropped me off at Darkwater: *If it is a matter of life and death, set this alight and the danger will be dealt with.*

Reed was pounding on my bedroom door. "I know you're in there, Margot!" he sang. I was out of time. I threw the bag in the fireplace, where a few glowing logs smoldered. It immediately caught fire and turned to ash right as Reed blew apart the bedroom door and began beating on the study.

Nothing came from the bag. No weapon, no monster. No protection. I tossed my coat on the ground so I might move more freely, then I grabbed a pen and hoped I could get a good shot in. If I could reach the point to his neck, I could stab him and make a break for it. I moved to hide but the door had already exploded into splinters.

I did my best to at least look defiant, even if I was shaking. Reed did not hesitate, did not stop to spew hate at me or tell me more of his plans. He marched forward and I raised my pen. He ripped it from my grasp and threw it aside before sending the back of his wounded hand across my face. The pain of the blow was tinted with the sharp sting of being hit with something cold and wet when his already congealing blood splattered on my cheek. I stayed on my feet for that first blow. The second had me reeling backward, and he sent his fist into my stomach, knocking the wind out of me and forcing me off my feet. My head made a nasty cracking noise when it struck the desk on the way down, and the immediate warmth on my hair and face told me I was bleeding. My ears were ringing, but that didn't stop my pathetic attempt at fighting Reed off when he stood over the top of me. "You could have been gone already," he said as he squatted down and poked the wound on my head, causing me to cry out. "But now it will be all too enjoyable to drag this out a bit longer."

"Fuck you," I wheezed. I spat at him and swelled with pride when it landed on his face. Reed wiped it away angrily before standing again to pull a knife from his belt. An evil grin spread across his face.

"I suppose now this will be my last chance to sample everything you refused me." He brought the tip of his knife to my bodice and sliced at it, exposing my breasts before going deeper still and slicing the skin between them. Warm blood pooled in the crevices of my chest and the cuts stung, but even being exposed like that, I did not truly grasp what Reed meant to do until he flipped me fully on my stomach. He used the same knife to cut open the back of my skirt clean up to my hips before sitting all his weight on top of me.

"No—" I croaked as fear and humiliation washed over me. "Reed, please—" He ignored me and fumbled with the front of his pants. I imagined his bloody fingers slipping on the buttons, delaying him. My breathing was labored, and my vision blurred. Fate's small kindness, I thought. Perhaps I would pass out before the worst of it.

I couldn't move. I couldn't scream. Even if I could, no one would hear me. No one was coming.

By what I could make out from behind me, Reed had freed himself, and I held my breath. My body tensed as I tried to prepare for what would come next.

And then a pair of boots strode silently beside my head. Was I hallucinating? Or worse, was this an accomplice of Reed's, come to aid in his ransacking once he'd raped and murdered me?

The boots passed swiftly, and then I could breathe a bit easier when Reed suddenly left his position sitting on me. I wanted to turn my head so I could see my death coming and face it head on, as if somehow that would improve the outcome, but the pain of everything was intense and sharp, and I was so tired. Everything sounded like I was underwater.

There was a heavy thud behind me. Perhaps the friend was getting started looking for valuables while Reed finished with me.

I felt my skirts being smoothed down to cover me again, and I gasped, flinching at the touch.

"Oh, thank the gods," a warm, familiar voice said loud enough that I had heard it. "I'm going to flip you over." I couldn't speak to respond, but a pained whimper escaped my lips when he did it.

Once I was on my back I could see Ever's stricken face, pale with worry. "Margot, honey, can you hear me?" He shrugged off his coat and spread it over my exposed body. I was shivering, and unable to believe my luck. I mustered up a single nod. "Good— good. I'm going to take you to get some help, alright? I have to carry you."

One more nod. "...Hurt," I whispered.

"I know, honey, I know you're hurt," Ever said gently, as he slid his arm under my knees. "I'm going to get you some help. Try to stay awake." His other arm went under my shoulders, and he stood in one fluid motion. Pain still seared through me as I jostled slightly. I was not going to stay awake.

My vision darkened at the edges, and I noticed the way the shadows formed around Ever, looking like wings. The last thing I remembered was Ever approaching the door, which in my stupor seemed to resemble a bright window. He stepped through it, and my mind slipped into blackness.

22

I was warm.

I was awake but had not yet opened my eyes. My lids felt as if they weighed a thousand pounds, and I was so comfortable— why not go back to sleep?

There were voices near enough that I could hear them, but far enough away that I couldn't quite make out what they were saying. Slowly, I opened my eyes, only managing to make it halfway. I could see the door from where I lay. Ever and Onyx were standing in the hallway. By the sharp looks on their faces and the way they each moved their hands as if to punctuate their statements, I could tell that they were arguing. Ever seemed to get the last word, pointing as if telling her to leave. Onyx froze for a moment before nodding in a slow way that almost looked like a bow. She turned on her heel and stormed off, leaving Ever alone where he stood. He took a deep breath before looking in my direction, and his expression immediately softened when he noticed I was awake, then his brows knit together, and he walked toward me carefully. "Margot?" It was then that I realized I was taking huge, gulping breaths. "Hey, you're alright— Margot, it's Ever. You're at my house—"

"Reed," I gasped, trying to settle down. "Reed has deceived me— he's got to be destroying Darkwater— Arlie and Vic—"

"They're here," Ever said gently. He sat down beside me on the edge of the bed. "I sent for them after I brought you home. It was Rhea who cleaned you up," he added, and then I noticed I was in a new nightdress. "When you feel up to it, I can send for a healer to come and give you a full assessment."

"How long have I been here?"

"Two days," he said. "Today would have been the third but it's quite early still."

"Where is Reed?" I asked.

Ever looked me over, sighed, and answered, "Reed Cypress is dead."

I took a single, deep breath and leaned back against the pillow with my eyes shut. "You killed him?"

"Yes."

Another beat. Another breath. "How."

"I ripped out his throat."

I took a second to adjust before I opened my eyes again. "Thank you," I whispered.

"Are you alright?" Ever asked.

"Yes— no. I—" I stammered, and my eyes welled. "Ever, I'm so sorry. I was so foolish— so fucking *stupid* to fall for his tricks. I saw your letters, and..." I trailed off, shaking my head. Ever took my hand in his and before I knew what I was doing, I started telling him everything: How I felt so abandoned and angry when my letters went unanswered and Reed swooping in to distract me. Our fight after I returned to the manor, and then everything that happened the day Reed died. Ever only reacted twice: first, when he heard about Reed's plan to blackmail him, his jaw stiffened. And second, when I relayed what I remembered about trying to fight Reed off, Ever's hold on my hand tightened just a fraction.

"Margot, I'm so sorry," he said when I was finished. "I hope you can see how brave you were."

"Brave?" I half laughed, wiping at my eyes with my free hand. "I'm an idiot, I'm not brave."

"You're not an idiot— or stupid, or foolish. Trusting people is not a character flaw, Margot. Especially when dealing with someone who cannot lie."

"It just seems, yet again, that I favor my human side," I said. "Trusting any faerie without further question is something a human would do, not the Lady of Sparrows."

Ever sighed. "You are so desperate to find a way to blame yourself for this, aren't you?"

"Who else would I blame?"

"Reed Cypress, for starters," he replied. "Then you can add me to the list."

"What do you mean?"

A pause. "I took a wife because I was commanded to," Ever said. "When I found you, I knew that our marriage could be mutually beneficial, and best of all, I actually liked you. I even... I wasn't sure why, but I hoped that, perhaps, despite the arrangement, we could be friends." His thumb ran across the back of my hand and I pretended not to notice. "Regardless, like I told you after we were wed, like you witnessed at the palace, I am not well liked by much of the royal family. I knew I would have to keep you safe, even if you never wanted to see me again after the wedding.

"I picked Darkwater because it would be the easiest to defend with the fewest number of sentries, so you would not be scared by their presence. I hired your sparse staff purposefully— and I knew that Reed Cypress aligned himself with anti-Avenist rebels."

"What?" I sputtered. "But— he forged his documents—"

"Poorly," Ever said. "I knew of Reed's reputation. I knew a few of his brothers were involved with the rebels as well. He made no effort to hide his true name, so none of this was difficult to discover. But I knew that while he held his position you would not be at risk of your staff selling you out to my family. The Cypresses would rather die than do favors for the palace. I can only guess that I was far enough down the line of succession that Reed did not deem it a disgrace to take my money. When your budding affair with him became clear, I was further assured of your safety. I did not anticipate that something like this could happen to you and that is purely my fault. My carelessness got you hurt."

I remained quiet long enough that Ever let go of my hand, giving me the space he thought I needed. After a moment, I took a deep breath. "If I'm not permitted to blame myself, you shouldn't be allowed to either."

Ever nodded, and we sat there together in silence for another moment before he spoke. "I have a few things I must do today, but I will arrange for a healer to come by this afternoon."

"I think I'd rather not," I said. "I don't want anyone else to know about it."

"There is no shame in this, Margot. Your injuries..."

"Are not extensive as Reed wanted them to be. They can be seen to by Rhea," I finished. "I feel alright, I promise. I just want to forget it."

Ever patted my hand. "Alright," he said. "Rhea will tend to you. But if she deems your injuries too severe for her, promise me you'll let her send for a healer?"

"Of course."

"And if you find you need someone to talk to about all of it, promise me you will let me know? Or Rhea, or Arlie—"

"I promise," I said. "If I need anything, you'll be the first to know." Satisfied with my answer, Ever moved to stand. "Ever?"

"Yes?" He sat again.

"How did you... what were you doing at Darkwater?" I asked. "It was so lucky that you found Reed and me at the perfect time, but why were you there?"

"You lit the spell," he said. "The white bag I gave you when I dropped you off."

I surprised us both by bursting into laughter. "*That's* what that was?" I asked. "I was expecting some weapon or monster to come flying out of the fireplace but it never came. I thought you'd given me a faulty charm."

"It did exactly as it was supposed to," Ever replied. "It alerted me that you were in grave danger. I dropped everything and sped to Darkwater."

"Did you have a travel spell on you? You got there so quickly."

"I will tell you some other time," Ever promised. "For now, I should get back to work. Is there anything else you need?"

"Well, no, but..." I started, then I felt stupid, so I said, "Nevermind."

"What is it?"

"Is it entirely necessary that I return to Darkwater right away?" I asked. "I know... Onyx told me that you're very busy, and I promise to make myself useful and not be a burden. I just—"

"You are welcome to stay as long as you want," Ever said. "This room, this house, and everything in it is as much yours as it is mine. It is your right."

"I know that," I replied. "But Onyx..."

"I have sent Onyx away for the time being," he said. "You won't have to worry about her opinions of my schedule and whether or not you impede upon it." He smirked a little, then added sincerely, "I would really like it if you stayed with me for a while, Margot."

"As long as I'm not being a bother."

"As long as you want," he said. "I could use the company."

"Okay," I said. "Thank you, Ever. For everything you've done."

"Don't mention it," he said. I yawned. "You should get some more rest."

"I've been asleep for two days—" I began to protest, but Ever stopped me.

"You've been through a lot, and you heal slower than fae medicine accounts for."

"But—"

"Rest, Margot. Please."

Defeated, I allowed Ever to help me lie back down. He pulled the blankets over me, tucking me in snugly before he stood. "Rhea will check on you in an hour. I'm down the hall if you need anything." Ever brushed a stray curl out of my face and smoothed his hand over my hair. Before he turned to leave, he bent down and brushed a soft kiss over my forehead. "Sleep well."

23

I grew stronger in the days that followed. Despite Rhea's fussing, insisting I rest longer, I hauled my body outside to get some sunshine the morning of the equinox.

I took the same spot by the tree that I read by months ago, and let my book lay flat in my lap. It was an adventure novel, from the human realm. A rare find, tucked away behind some other volumes in Ever's study. Within an hour, I was immersed in the story, even when strange words I did not recognize went over my head.

I lifted my head when the sound of boots tracking through the yard met my ears. Ever approached, his hands tucked casually into his pockets. "Mind if I join you?" he asked.

"Not at all." I patted the ground beside me, gesturing for him to sit. He took up a spot beside me, pressing his back against the golden trunk and tilting his head upward to let the sun kiss his face.

"Lucky us," he said quietly after a few moments. "We are witness to the leaves turning back."

I turned to Ever, not knowing what he meant, and followed his finger when he pointed at the branches spreading above us. Indeed, the leaves, which had been all shades of blue through the autumn and winter, were darkening to shades of violet, mauve, and plum. I felt the corners of my mouth tug upward, remembering my sorrow all those months ago at the thought of never seeing this. So much had changed since then.

Ever's observation did not require an answer, and so I did not provide one beyond a smile, before returning to my book. We enjoyed the silence together, until the sound of rowdy voices began ringing out from beyond the tree line, laughing and singing songs in some old language or another. I recognized the rustling at the tops of the trees as the party tricks of woodsprites.

"Revelers," Ever provided without opening his eyes. "Celebrating the equinox. They're from the village a few miles west. I let them use the woods and the grounds up to the wards for their celebrations each year. Bonfires and fireworks don't mix well with the town square."

"I can imagine," I said with some amusement.

"Would you like to join them?" Ever asked.

"I don't— er, no. No, I don't think so," I stammered.

"No problem." My husband shrugged. His eyes opened and he faced me, grinning. "But we should head inside, or else the fishermen will insist we drink with them. Trust me when I say I've fallen victim to their persistence more than once." Ever stood and offered his hand to help me to my feet.

We ate a quiet dinner together, my tastebuds alert at the addition of early springtime vegetables and fresh lemberry tarts for dessert. The grounds outside of the house's wards were aglow with bonfires, and through the open windows we could hear their drinking songs growing more slurred as the night went on. The berrywine, it seemed, had no problem flowing tonight. Ever even told Rhea to send a case outside from his own private stores, as a gift to the revelers. I had bid everyone goodnight and was changing for bed when I heard their distant cheers and knew the gifted wine had been received.

I was about to put out my lamp when a knock sounded on my bedroom door. I answered and found Ever there, with the book I'd been reading that afternoon in his hands.

"You left this outside," he said, offering it to me. "I thought you might want it, if you felt like reading before bed."

"Oh," I said, taking it from him. "I didn't realize I walked off without it. Thank you."

"Of course," Ever replied. "It's excellent, though I'm sure you've figured that out by now. One of my favorites."

"I am enjoying it very much, yes."

A pause. "I won't keep you any longer. Just wanted to drop that off and wish you goodnight." With a small smile, he turned toward his own door.

"Would you—" I started, causing Ever to stop in his tracks. "Would you want to stay and read it with me?"

"Read it with you?"

"Yes," I said, feeling a flush stain my cheeks as soon as the words left my lips. "My friends and I, when I was younger, back in Sparrow Court, rather than wait for one person to be done with a book we all liked before the next could read it, we would gather and read aloud to one another, so we could all enjoy the story at once." A smile tugged at Ever's lips. "It's silly, I know, I just thought—"

"I think I would love that," Ever replied before I could finish. I stepped aside for him to enter. He pulled my vanity chair to my bedside so he could sit, and then insisted I at least sit on the bed instead of letting him conjure another chair, and risk Rhea scolding them for letting me exert myself too much in one day.

Picking up from where I left off, I began reading to Ever, not stopping even when my eyes began to grow too heavy to concentrate. When I began truly dozing off, Ever took the book from my hands and began reading in my stead. His warm voice continued the story, caressing my senses as I fell just beyond the waking world, where I could still hear and feel my surroundings. After a few minutes, Ever fell quiet, and I knew he had noticed my sleeping state. I felt him pull the amethyst quilt over my body before setting the book on my bedside table. His hand smoothed my hair out of my face, stroking just once before he turned out my lamp and left.

The sounds of the equinox celebration grew more distant as I slipped deeper into true sleep. Quiet contentment filled me, and in the safety of my husband's home, my mind carried me into a night of gentle oblivion.